PACHA ALIVE APP

Bring book to life!

1. Turn on Wi-Fi
2. Install Pacha Alive app
3. Hover device over an image

Visit http:/app.pachaspajamas.com

PRAISE FOR PACHA

"It's good to give children a sense of the importance of the environment around them—not just nature but the general environment. Shout-out to *Pacha's Pajamas* and everyone involved!"

— **Yasiin Bey fka Mos Def**, Rapper and Actor

"*Pacha's Pajamas* is a wonderful creative introduction to understanding the sacred connection we as human beings must now acknowledge. By giving voice to the plants and animals, the story creates awareness of LIFE beyond the human being."

— **Mona Polacca**, International Council of Indigenous Grandmothers

"This story about a little girl's dream—where all species unite to support a healthy planet — will play a catalytic role in building our movements for change. Please invite everyone you know to buy this book!"

— **Van Jones**, Author of The Green Collar Economy

"A beautiful story for both children and adults to help us all visualize the world that can be."

— **David Korten**, Author of The Great Turning
and Agenda for a New Economy

"*Pacha's Pajamas* will open the minds and hearts of countless children, introducing them to the magic of Mother Nature in her wondrous manifestations as plants, stones, animals. A must 'read and share' with all you know."

— **Michael Bernard Beckwith**, Author of Spiritual Liberation

"*Pacha's Pajamas* is a fun, creative and beautiful way to engage children of all ages in helping reconnect with the Earth that is our home and all of the life that we share our home with."

"*Pacha's Pajamas* is a fun story that will inspire kids to become leaders in promoting greater connection with Nature. What could be more important? Grounded in a deep-time, ecological worldview, this children's book deserves a wide readership."

"I love Pacha's Pajamas because of the empowering message it gives children about their future and the environment. I often sense that the children I speak to shut down a little when they hear of environmental calamities. But this engaging story of a sweet but strong heroine coming together in song with the animal kingdom is of great value in helping kids feel able to affect their world. My own children immediately gravitated towards the cover and had questions about Pacha. The story speaks to their need for an environmental hero, and they quickly saw themselves in her. I am also very excited to have the Pacha's Pajamas CD and book as a tool in reaching out to my patients about the importance of nature in their lives. As a pediatrician, I understand the accumulating scientific evidence that kids must get outdoors and into nature for their health. How to get them there is always the dilemma. Artists and entertainers are invaluable partners in the healer's quest to engage kids in the natural world. "

"*Pacha's Pajamas* is an eloquently written and timely fable that will not only inspire children AND adults to DREAM of a healthier, more sustainable planet, but also inspire them to TAKE ACTION!"

— **Joel Harper**, Author of *All the Way to the Ocean*

"I love watching Pacha as she demonstrates her joyful dance of connection, and then, in her story, shows how one imaginative child can help save our planet. Pacha's fascinating adventures will go into the hearts of young and old across the world; the story will lift spirits and bring smiles. Enjoy and pass it on."

— **Seena B. Frost**, Founder of the SoulCollage® process and author of SoulCollage® Evolving.

"Pacha's Pajamas is the children's book series we've all been waiting for—a gift for teachers, parents, and anyone who engages with young people. Reading Pacha's Pajamas reignited my imagination! It's a heartfelt, inspirational story with unforgettable characters and imagery as well as a fun and relevant way of introducing social emotional learning, civic engagement, and eco-literacy to young people."

— **Meena Srinivasan**, author of Teach, Breathe, Learn: Mindfulness In and Out of the Classroom & Program Manager, Social Emotional Learning & Leadership—Oakland Unified School District

"Pacha's Pajamas is a wonderful illustration showing how self-care is tied to earth care. The story introduces kids to not only self-awareness but also earth awareness. Kids, teachers, parents and guardians alike will be instantly charged with becoming ambassadors of the world to help make it a healthier and better place to live."

— **Marcus Lorenzo Penn**, M.D., C.Y.T., Holistic Physician, Self Care Coach, Health/Wellness Consultant

Special Guest

Express yourself!

Scan here for instructions
on placing your Augmented
video here

A Story Written by Nature

Aaron Ableman
and Dave Room

New York

PACHA'S PAJAMAS
A Story Written by Nature

Published in New York, New York, by Morgan James Publishing. Morgan James is a trademark of Morgan James, LLC. www.MorganJamesPublishing.com

The Morgan James Speakers Group can bring authors to your live event. For more information or to book an event visit The Morgan James Speakers Group at www.TheMorganJamesSpeakersGroup.com.

ISBN 978-1-63047-704-2 paperback
ISBN 978-1-63047-705-9 eBook
Library of Congress Control Number: 2015911433

Illustrations by:
Allah El Henson & Michelle Fang

Cover Design by:
Allah El Henson and
Rachel Lopez, www.r2cdesign.com

Interior Design by:
Bonnie Bushman
The Whole Caboodle Graphic Design

In an effort to support local communities, raise awareness and funds, Morgan James Publishing donates a percentage of all book sales for the life of each book to Habitat for Humanity Peninsula and Greater Williamsburg.

Get involved today! Visit
www.MorganJamesBuilds.com

This book is dedicated to all the kids around the world
still dreaming, singing, and living
in harmony with nature.

"There can be no keener revelation of a society's soul
than the way in which it treats its children."
— **Nelson Mandela**

PROLOGUE

I t was one of those days. Warm and balmy. The perfect day for a nap if only it wasn't a school day.

Pacha sat under the only tree in her school playground, reading a book about a strange animal called a platypus. The egg-laying, duck-billed, beaver-tailed, otter-footed mammal was unlike anything Pacha had ever imagined.

She wanted to learn everything she could about platypuses before lunch was over. Next period, Pacha had to give a report on this crazy creature. She was nervous about talking in front of the whole class. But figured if she really knew her stuff, she'd get through it.

Yet Pacha was having a hard time focusing. The heat rising off the concrete made her eyes droopy and her thoughts mushy.

She drifted into a daydream about meeting a platypus at the edge of a river.

The platypus told her that no matter who you are, you must "use what you got" to bring your dreams to life. He said his dream was to keep the rivers cool...he didn't want his family to be fried platypi! And he also taught her the Duck Dance!

The bell rang. Pacha woke up and hurried back to her classroom. "The ice caps are melting," she told the class. "And the rivers and oceans are heating up, which is making life hard for platypuses and other animals."

Her classmates looked puzzled. Pacha decided to try something else. "Um...have you ever thought about what it would be like to live in a world without ice cream?!"

"That doesn't make any sense," her classmate Aaron said, and everyone laughed.

Pacha was embarrassed, yet something inside her had awakened, a force of nature beyond words.

CHAPTER 1

LITTLE GIRL, BIG DREAMS

P acha was a little girl with big dreams. Her dreams were bigger than the biggest elephant at the zoo. Her dreams were bigger than the Andes Mountains, the homeland of her parents and ancestors. She dreamed of lost secrets and upside-down rainbows. She dreamed of dancing in front of huge crowds. But her biggest dream was for everyone to come together.

Sadly, real life wasn't so dreamy. Maybe it was the hazy weather lately that made it hard to breathe. Maybe it was the plastic bag that looked like it was dancing in the wind. That AND she had to perform the Earth Day musical tomorrow!

Sometimes life seemed easier when she hid in her room, frozen in time like a frog under a winter lake.

When Pacha and her father got home from school, she started wheezing and coughing, and her toes scrunched up in pain.

"I can't breathe! I...feel like...Ms. Wheezer blew a hurricane down my throat!"

Ms. Wheezer was a name that she had given her breathing problem, trying to make it sound as silly as she could so it wouldn't scare her. But that didn't work this time; this felt like the worst attack ever.

With blue lips, she huffed and puffed. Her father calmed her by cuddling her in his arms, encouraging her to let the attack pass like clouds in the sky. She took a deep draw on the inhaler her father handed her and finally found her breath. As if right on time, her mother entered the front door.

Pacha's mother set the groceries on the floor. "*Amor*, did you have another attack?"

Pacha fell into her mother's arms and cried: "Why does this happen to me?!"

"*Ai mi vida*, I know this is so hard for you," her mother responded calmly, "but let's remember that struggling only makes it worse. If you see life like a dream, even nightmares can't take you off track!"

But Pacha was still sobbing. "Can you ask Ms. Wheezer to get a new job? I'm sick of being sick!"

"Well, I wish I could fire Ms. Wheezer... but I do have something that could help you feel better...something for you to wear like a hero's cape, especially on nights like tonight."

With that, Pacha's mother brought out a colorful pair of pajamas, which looked like they were glowing. They were covered with dancing animals and singing plants. "These are magical pajamas!" her mother said. "When I was your age, my mother made me pajamas woven from baby alpaca fleece—a fabric of royalty and medicine people. **She told me that every stitch was a prayer, giving thanks to Pachamama.**"

"¡Ai, *Mamá!* They're as soft as a chinchilla's belly!" Pacha exclaimed as she giggled for the first time all day. **Hugging her mother and feeling a tingle in her heart, Pacha closed her eyes.** She imagined the PJs were a special friend or a magic carpet carrying her to distant lands. Perhaps this pair of jammies could be her new dreamcatcher?

That evening, as Pacha put on her new PJs, she had a funny feeling that her life was changing. What's more, she had lots of questions for her father.

"Does the sky breathe?" she wondered. "Does it choke on all the smoke and storms in the air these days? And before people, did animals make the rules?"

Pacha paused as her eyes rested on an old gorilla mask on the shelf near her bed. She had worn it for the Halloween performance last year. She had forgotten her lines, but there was no worrying about that now. Putting it on, she danced like a goofy gorilla, exclaiming, "Can I be a dancing girl-illa in these pajamas?" as if all her problems had gone away. Her father laughed. "So many questions, *mi angelita.* **Maybe if you jump in bed faster than a little jaguar, you will find the answers in your dream.**"

Pacha stuffed the gorilla mask into her pajama pocket, snuggled into bed, and drifted away.

CHAPTER 2

TROUBLE IN THE WATERS

It all began when a whale shouted to a hummingbird—something that doesn't happen in just any dream.

"Help! Help! I'm drowning!" yelled the whale.

The crimson-chested hummingbird stopped midair and hovered above the splashing beneath her. Pacha was hiding behind a tree near the shore, shocked by what she was seeing. When the whale cried again, Pacha felt a choke in her own throat! "I wish I could help that whale but I can barely breathe myself," she thought.

FUN FACT

Are hummingbirds magical?

Hummingbirds can dive at 60 miles per hour—that's as fast as a car driving on the highway! Because of their speed, they are known as messengers and time stoppers. To keep up their energy, hummingbirds need to eat every 15 to 20 minutes. They feed off hundreds of flowers per day, drinking their nectar and pollinating the next flower they visit (helping the flowering plants to produce seeds). Hummingbirds are the only birds that can fly backward, forward, up, down and sideways, and even hover in the air! They teach us to let the past go and appreciate the magic of the present moment. Legends say the hummingbird is a messenger between worlds, spreading joy, healing, and sweetness during times of great change. In many cultures, hummingbird feathers are prized for their magical powers.

• •

"Something is stuck in my blowhole!" the whale gasped.

Pacha wheezed into the soft folds of her PJs. She wanted to help the whale but felt woozy and helpless.

FUN FACT

What are whale songs?

Whales use sound and calling to communicate. The whale belly is a special place for hearing and feeling the music of the oceans. The largest whales can send a call, or song, around the entire planet's oceans and speak directly to another whale on the other side of the world! Smaller toothed whales also use sound and calling to "see." This is called echolocation. The sounds bounce off other objects or animals to tell the whale the shape, distance, and texture of its surroundings. In many cultures, whales represent creativity and intuition. They can also symbolize the regenerative cycle of death and rebirth.

• •

Despite her discomfort, Pacha was amazed to hear these animals speaking in her language. The only animals she'd ever heard talk were beatboxing parrots and singing goats. Pacha squinted as the tiny hummingbird peered into the hole on top of the whale's head. Using her tiny beak, the colorful bird pulled out a plastic bag.

The whale spouted a huge jet of water and took a deep breath. "Thank you for saving my life! You never know how nice it is to breathe...until you can't. Have my kind lived for over 50 million years just to wash ashore with sea trash? But please let me introduce myself...my name is Wilder the Whale, the baritone-bass in the Seven Seas whale choir!"

"You're most welcome, Wilder. My friends call me Hum. I'd say you're one lucky whale. I have always loved whales. I never knew little ol' me could help someone like you. Sometimes I feel powerless when I'm facing big problems...but I can't let that stop me!"

Pacha smirked, watching as Hum zipped above a branch of the tree she was hiding behind.

"I've never seen this planet in such bad shape!" Hum said. "Birds everywhere are fighting over scraps of garbage! Just the other day, an albatross friend of mine discovered an island of trash floating in the ocean that looked bigger than Buenos Aires! What's happening?"

Hum started to cry little hummingbird tears. "I can't figure it out! Even the bees of the PolliNation are disappearing by the bazillions...what do we do?"

Pacha wondered if she should join the troubled animals or stay out of sight for a bit longer. She wanted to help, but didn't want to startle them. It was a good thing she kept hiding, because out of nowhere, a jaguar appeared in a suit and tie. The jaguar looked awful, with tufts of hair missing from his body.

"Jag, what's wrong?" Hum asked. "You look miserable!"

The burly cat sniffed the wind, raised his hazel green eyes to the sky, and cleared his throat. "The planet is angry and so am I! I've been running along the edge of the rainforest for hours without a drop of water all day. Every time I stopped for a drink I was chased off..."

FUN FACT

What's special about the jaguar?

The jaguar is an important creature that helps to keep nature in balance. Quick and agile, the jaguar is the largest of the big cats in the Americas. A majestic animal found in habitats ranging from desert to rainforest, this big cat is threatened by hunting and habitat loss. The jaguar is loved in traditional cultures for its spotted coat, and stories have told of its skin magically forming the heavens and stars. A symbol of courage, the jaguar represents the power to face one's fears and confront one's enemies with love.

• •

"But let me not forget," the big cat said changing the subject. "I bring news from the Organization of Organized Organisms. There is war... between the hungry and the hungry-for-more. The jungle is shrinking day by day and something in the air is making the weather act strange. If things keep going this way," said the feline, ripping off his tie. "I may lose my job! Time, like the rain that fills our watering holes, is running out."

Pacha wanted to join the animals, but she worried that as a human they might blame her for their problems. Plus, when she spoke up in groups, she often felt like a squeaky mouse in a crowd of elephants. So rather than introduce herself, she climbed the tree and watched silently from atop a branch.

Just then, Pebble cracked out from a boulder in the grass. "Ya'll think you have it bad?" he shouted. "There's a crack in my heart and it's getting wider every day! My friends are being blown up and ripped away from their underground families. They're traded, used up, and thrown away—and I can't do anything about it because I'm just another sandstone fighting to keep myself together! We can't just wait around, watching the world fall apart grain by grain..."

Moaning like a ghost from an old haunted house, Tree creaked into the conversation. "I have problems too, but mine are worse than a spider monkey on a bad hair day!"

FUN FACT

Have you ever heard a tree talk?

Reaching down into the ground and up to the sky at the same time, trees represent life, growth, antiquity and strength. Some trees actually "talk" or "sing" to each other. When a willow tree is attacked by caterpillars or webworms, it lets off a natural chemical that warns other trees nearby of danger. The other trees then start pumping a chemical called tannin into their leaves, making it difficult for insects to swallow the leaves. Trees also can bring on the rain by a process called transpiration—they cool the land by drinking water through their roots and then release that water into the sky through invisible openings in their leaves. And did you know that one fully grown, leafy tree can provide enough oxygen for ten people to breathe for a whole year?

• •

When Pacha realized that she was sitting in a talking tree, she almost choked on her tongue. She wanted to jump down, but that would have revealed her to the animals, which she wasn't ready to do.

"All we trees do is give, give, give—and we receive so little in return! I just hope that I don't end up another dead stump like so many of my aunts and uncles. Whatever happened to a simple thank you? This is supposedly the year of the forest, but it seems more like the year of the saw."

A terrified shiver went through the tree, shaking Pacha to her core. Pacha looked around to get her bearings in case she needed to jump. When she looked down, she saw that the old toy gorilla mask had fallen out of her pocket and onto the ground. "Oh, no!" she thought. "If one of the animals sees the mask, they might discover me."

Pacha was overcome by danger below and stormy clouds above. She was out of breath again. She felt the inhaler in her pocket, but that might blow her cover. She longed for her parents. If Mama were here, she'd flip Pacha's frown rightside up. And if Papa were here, he'd say something that would help her see ways out of the situation. Or at least remind her to calm herself by counting her breaths backwards from five to one.

Just as Pacha was feeling she would blow her top, a mushroom popped up from the earth. "Why is everybody so down in the dumps? All things can change, and I can change ANYTHING! I am Señor Champignón and I can turn plastic into guacamole! I can change trash into compost to feed the gardens and help the forests regrow!"

With that, a stray gust of wind blew down through Tree's branches, nearly knocking Pacha down. She was struck in the shoulder by one of Tree's limbs. At first she thought it was a gust of wind, but then it crossed her mind that the Tree might be mad at her. Maybe the Tree didn't like a primate in pajamas? Pacha tried her best to avoid the branches thrashing about her. Just as she was stepping towards another branch, her pajamas snagged and she lost her footing...

CHAPTER 3

MR. TICK

In the grasses down below, someone else was having a bad day too. A lowly tick lumbered onto the stage wondering, of all times, why a "fire drill" had to happen during his big moment, the grand gathering of the Parasites. How could it be that just when everyone gathered on the grass, a huge gorilla fell from the sky, causing everyone to lose their marbles? Much to Mr. Tick's frustration, the mask was now blocking the main pathway to the outdoor theater. Once everyone was finally more or less assembled, Mr. Tick grabbed a microphone, apologized for the disruption, and launched into his story.

"When I was just a young tick, I wished I could be a bedbug and bite humans. In my teens, I wanted to be a cockroach and eat the crumbs on the kitchen counter—more variety. In my adulthood, I worked to spread my fame like a virus. But now that I'm older, I am happy to be a simple

tick." He huffed and puffed with his sagging belly. "We ticks, like good parasites, bypass human food and go straight for the jugular!"

The crowd of parasites erupted in a scary chant: "Juggalo! Juggalo! Juggalo!"

Mr. Tick talked like a smarty-pants and yelled to get his point across. "Parasites! We know we have done well with the rise of humans! But with the help of other species who also benefit from humans, we can keep this gravy train going!

"Today we are overjoyed to welcome several high-level ambassadors from the rodent kingdom. They are thinking about my proposal for a truce between all species that live better with humans than without them. Thank you again for being here." Mr. Tick gestured to three elderly blind mice in dark overcoats and sunglasses near the front. He huffed and puffed again, "Do you have any messages for the Parasites from the great order of Rodentia?"

One of the mice hopped onto her lounge chair. "We bring many greetings and good tidings on behalf of mice, rats, and squirrels everywhere. We, like you parasites, thrive in human cities where we live fatter than in the wild. In the outback, you just can't order a burger and fries, if you know what I mean. We are excited to see what you are proposing. *Danke!*"

"With the help of our rodent friends, we can bring the dogs and cats onboard, which will seal the deal!" Mr. Tick shouted when the cheering died down. "With your support, we will keep the human population growing." His fat belly rubbed against the microphone, making a grumbling sound that echoed through the theater.

"Seven billion humans and counting!" Mr. Tick continued. "This is a good thing not only for parasites, but for rodents and all species who live off of these fearful yet strangely powerful two-legged critters. Curiously, if humans keep growing, small will become the new big!"

Roars of ticks, rodents, wasps, lice, bedbugs, and fleas thundered across the grassy knoll.

"You make a great point, Mr. Tick," a tapeworm shouted. "We parasitic worms love the new varieties of human available these days! The large human tastes like bacon; the little human tastes like candy. My favorite flavor is french fries—I smell them a mile away!"

"That's right!" said Mr. Tick. "Just imagine eating as much as you like, whenever you like, whatever you like—whomever you like. Doooo whaaaatya like! Freedom is knowing where your next meal is coming from! We can create a New Food Order! As the human footprint grows, so shall we!"

"NFO! NFO! NFO!" the crowd chanted.

Mr. Tick picked up two baby plants and raised them over his head. "These are the new kings of the plant kingdom! They fatten up more people than anything. Yes, parasites and rodents, I am talking about

NEW corn and NEW soybean. These plants will make our dreams come true!"

But just as he said that, he heard a gasp from above, and looked up to see a human slipping from a tree branch and—as if in slow-motion—falling toward him. Pacha crashed directly on top of Mr. Tick, scattering the entire event into chaos.

CHAPTER 4

THE MASK

The drama continued all around Pacha as she collected herself from the fall and got up gingerly.

Hum swooped down to see what had happened. The hummingbird was shocked and concerned. But when Pacha looked up at Hum with tears in her eyes, it was like family.

"Are you ok, *nena*?" the bird whispered. "I'm the only one who knows your secret. As long as you quickly put on the mask, you'll be alright... everyone knows gorillas often hang out in trees."

The gorilla mask was smiling at Pacha from a couple feet away. Pacha grabbed the mask, strapped it on, and with Hum's help, nudged it perfectly in place.

Then Pacha felt a prick on her hand! She looked down and saw a bug trying to burrow into her thumb! When Pacha saw the critter, she squealed like a hog on its way to a hootenanny.

"What are you doing, you crazy faker!" it screeched. "You can't stop the one and only Mr. Tick!"

Hum snarled. "If you ever try to harm her again, I'll spear you with my beak and eat you for dinner!"

Mr. Tick went cross-eyed with anger, but then he let go of Pacha's hand. "She just ruined my entire life," he pouted. "The very least I can do is ruin hers!"

Then Mr. Tick spewed a wicked rhyme at Pacha:

"Fee-fi-fo-fum,
I smell the blood of a human one,
As she lives, until she's dead
She'll rue the day she saw my head."

This prompted some severe questioning from Jag and Pebble, who seemed suspicious of a little gorilla in pajamas. Pacha held her breath, terrified that she would be discovered as the large cat sniffed her down. But her pajamas must have smelled funky, because Jag backed off immediately.

Señor Champiñón suggested there were more important things to do than question a little gorilla in pajamas! While the rest of the group shifted their attention to Señor, Hum hovered over Pacha. The little gorilla didn't say a word for fear that Jag or the tired old tree would notice her human accent. They didn't seem to like humans—much less humans pretending to be animals!

Hum and Pacha, with an angry Mr. Tick on her shoulder, joined the circle around Tree, and the group continued talking. Hum taught Wilder the Whale some birdcalls. Tree showed off her fluent mushroom with Señor, and Jag showed Pebble how to roar. Pacha and Mr. Tick were having a fierce staring contest. Then Señor proposed they talk about change.

"But what about everyone who doesn't want change?" Pebble asked.

"Yeah, what about the ones who like the way things are going?" Mr. Tick added.

"I am going to answer your questions with a question," Señor said. "What did the teacher say to the vegan hot dog vendor?"

The others didn't have a clue. "Make me one with everything!"

Led by Señor, the group had a hearty laugh. Thankful for a moment of silliness, Pacha giggled, imagining a mushroom ordering a vegan hot dog.

"The hot dog vendor gave him the hot dog with everything on it but didn't give him his change," Señor continued. "The teacher asked, 'Wait, where's my change?' and the hot dog vendor said, 'Change comes from within!'"

The creatures chuckled and smirked. Pacha was amused but feeling out of breath and a little sick to her tummy.

"But...but...Señor...you said that all things can change! What does that even mean?" Pacha asked.

This question seemed to excite the mushroom and he lit up like a firefly. "It means...all things come and go, like clouds en el cielo!"

"But what does that have to do with us?"

"It means we need to look at the bigger picture! We need to do something together, something really, really special—bigger than when my cousin Myco performed for the entire Mycelial network. How can we change ourselves and not change the world? Real change comes in many ways, from the inside or the outside, from good times or from challenges—but the biggest changes happen when we start working together!"

CHAPTER 5

THE BIG IDEA

W ell, if you want to change the world, you're going to have to fight for it!" Mr. Tick said.

"Aren't you a pest?" Señor Champigñón chuckled. "Can't you see that Wilder is catching his breath, Hum is jumpy, Jag is angry, Pebble is heartbroken, and Tree is worried sick? Not to mention, the little gorilla in pajamas looks like it swallowed a frog! We don't need anymore fighting! We already have enough problems!"

At that, the entire group erupted like a volcano.

"I am concerned about the family tree; we are the lungs of the earth!" said Tree, waving her branches with the wind.

"We need to clean up the oceans and the rivers. Water is the blood of the planet," spouted Wilder.

"Why can't we protect our climate? Let's keep Pachamama happy. Our livelihoods depend on it!" said Jag, stroking his furry chin.

"Let's keep the tops on mountains and the oil in the soil!" said Pebble.

"I think we need more things to eat at the buffet line!" said Mr. Tick, speaking out of the side of his mouth.

Pacha coughed and choked, feeling dizzy.

"I think we need to change the diapers of the world," said Señor Champignón, winking at the ground.

Hum zipped around the entire group. "We need to overcome our selfish ways," she said, lifting an eyebrow at Mr. Tick. "We also need to learn to listen to one another," she said to the others.

But they were all talking at once; no one heard what anyone else was saying. Pacha felt like she was in a bad movie in a foreign language. She began to sob. Her breath grew worse and she began to pant for air. Finally, when she couldn't take it anymore, she screamed out:

"AAACK! Help! Help!"

FUN FACT

How amazing are mushrooms?

Mushrooms were among the first living things to move onto land from the ocean. They began to live on land 1.3 billion years ago, 600 million years before plants. Can you say mycoremediation (my-co-re-midi-ay-shun)? It is a process in which mushroom roots, called mycelium, break down pollutants of all kinds, like heavy metals, plastics, and chemicals, and remove them from the environment. Mushrooms are sacred, medicinal, and have been revered by numerous civilizations throughout history. Not to mention, one of the largest living things on the planet is the "honey" mushroom that has been growing in Oregon for 2,400 years and spreads over 2,200 acres. That's the size of 1,665 football fields!

• •

All of the others stopped talking at once and turned to Lil Gorilla. Concerned, they rushed to her side and comforted her. Hum flapped some fresh air toward her. After a few moments of sweaty palms, Pacha began to breathe easier.

Señor Champignón was the first to speak. "¡Ay caramba! Life is too precious to choke on it. Even if the situation smells like rotten eggs with old mustard, it's really just time to make compost!"

"I think that when you have a problem, just fight your way out of it!" Mr. Tick said. "Life sucks, like a bad party with straws and no drinks, but the secret to winning wars is getting started!"

As if struck by lightning, the mushroom responded by jumping almost a foot off the ground, and turned the colors of the rainbow. "I totally disagree! I think that a *fiesta* might be an answer for changing this world! Of course, changing the diapers of the world will require us to work together, but can you think of a better way of working together than having a party?"

The creatures looked at each other curiously. Nobody argued that they didn't like a good party. Lil Gorilla was first to smile, then the wee bird, followed by Pebble, Wilder, and Tree. Some even laughed as Lil Gorilla lightly hummed MJ's Thriller.

"Growing up in the barrios between two concrete slabs, I had to learn how to be a fun guy!" Señor Champignón continued. "I found out that if you want to get people's attention, you have to throw a fabulous *fiesta!*"

The group bounced with excitement. Pebble and Señor spun in place. Hum zipped around Tree, who took deep breaths and swayed in the breeze. Jag and Lil Gorilla roared like crazy. Everyone smiled with their beaks, fangs, or whatever else they had to smile with. Everyone except Mr. Tick.

Pebble cracked his back and stretched. "Can you help me understand your larger message, Señor? I'm sorry, but sometimes I'm a little dense."

"I share all of these ideas with you because I've learned that even when we're scared, sick, and don't know how to change," the mushroom responded, "we can always do something to make life a little better for someone else."

The mushroom popped up again and shouted so loud that even the sleepy whale jumped up with a splash.

"I think we need to...throw a Nature Festival!"

CHAPTER 6

THE SPIRIT OF THE EARTH

The creatures had mixed feelings about the idea. Pebble was weighing the option heavily. Lil Gorilla and Hum wondered how they could create something out of nothing. Jag and Tree seemed worried about whether this would be just another festival where everybody forgets why they came. Mr. Tick was ticked-off by the crazy idea and ready to start a royal rumble instead.

Just then, Pacha noticed that something stirring in the grass had caught Mr. Tick's attention. It was a mob of parasites and wasps that had avoided Pacha's fall. They were watching the group intensely.

"What are they are doing here?" Pacha wondered, imagining ticks on lounge chairs at the beach sucking on people's necks with long straws. She noticed Mr. Tick wink towards the parasites.

"What in the world is a Nature Festival?" Tree was the first to ask out loud.

"A Nature Festival is a concert for all species to sing and dance together!" exclaimed Señor. "It's also a place for plants and animals to share and enjoy the miracle of music, art, and conversations about how to help Pachamama. It might be our last chance to unite all species and create a better future!"

Hum whizzed around, aflutter with excitement. "Maybe the eagle and the condor can have a duet."

Just then a platypus splashed up from the river at the edge of the forest. He looked familiar to Pacha but she couldn't remember from where. "If you guys are having a party, can I perform one of my songs?"

"I don't know about all of this!" Tree said. "It could be a disaster trying to get billions of crazy creatures together. What if the pine beetles eat all of the trees? Plus, the mosquitoes will bother everyone! And what if a hurricane comes? I don't think I can go through with this. Unless we can create some very real ways to solve problems, it's just going to be another silly party."

"Maybe instead of having just one big party, we could also have different groups focused on solving problems!" Señor said. "We could have a stage for each biome. We'd have a stage in a swamp or a marsh, a coral reef, and a river or an estuary. We'd have a farm stage. We'd have stages in savannahs, temperate forests and grasslands, the jungle, tundra, the ocean, and a desert.

"And I know the perfect place where all these biomes come together," the mushroom continued. "That's where our festival could be. That way we can all come together for the main show, and species that share a biome home or the same problem can figure out what they can do to turn things around! We draw them in with music and dancing on the Main Stage, and then put them to work on solving their problems with their neighbors on the biome stages."

"Sounds like a gigantic amount of work, even to me," said Wilder the Whale slowly with a huge spouting sigh.

"Why are you two scared of standing up for something you believe in or diving deep for what you love?" Pebble snapped. "I'm with Señor on this. Everything CAN change! I was once a huge boulder, now I'm just a small stone. Someday, I'll be sand! Together, we can move mountains. It may be hard, but I'm ready to rock, y'all!"

FUN FACT

Who is Pachamama?

Pachamama is a goddess revered by the indigenous peoples of the Andes Mountains. Pachamama means Mother Earth. In the language of Aymara and Quechua, mama means "mother," and pacha means "world," "land," or "the cosmos." Pachamama and her father, Inti, are some of the most important gods from the Inca Empire, which stretched from present-day Peru through Ecuador and Chile to Argentina. In Inca mythology, Mama Pacha, or Pachamama, is a fertility goddess who watches over planting and harvesting. She can cause earthquakes and great change.

• •

The jaguar howled. "Long ago, when I was a cub, my mama told me that where I'm from, the Spirit of Nature is known as Pachamama. Long ago, Pachamama was connected to all of her children and life was in balance. But now, she is quite sick. Pachamama is calling to us!"

Jag's words awakened long-forgotten memories and stories from Pacha's childhood. She imagined her brightly dressed abuelita cradling her while singing stories about Pachamama. She recalled her mother telling her that Pacha was named after Mother Earth. She remembered her father chuckling and calling her "Pachamamasita" when she used to play in the dirt and jump in mud puddles.

The memories awoke something in Pacha. Chills moved from the earth to her feet up through her legs to her heart.

"We can't have the trees worrying about pine beetles, hummingbirds worrying about hawks, or gorillas worrying about ticks," Jag continued. "We must do something never done before—we need to stop fighting and eating one another. We need peace! We need a worldwide truce for the entire nature festival!"

Señor seconded the motion and called for "Ayes." Everyone agreed except Mr. Tick, who didn't vote, saying "the First Rule of Parasites is don't kill your host."

When the vote was done, Pacha noticed a tiny spider gliding down from the tree.

The other creatures fell silent as the spider cleared her throat. "Call me Auntie Sage. I have heard you speaking of an earth party to reconnect the world wide web of life. If so, I'd like to give it a spin. This won't be so easy, but it does seem like an idea whose time has come!"

The entire group watched hypnotized as Auntie Sage wove a web that looked like the planet Earth from space. She showed how the earth was out of balance. "Close your eyes to see!" she said. "Breathe in to breathe out. Whatever problems you have, let them go for now! Be a warrior for peace, not a worrier...please! The only thing that is constant is change!"

For the first time all day, everyone started to relax. Pacha got a tingly feeling in her body. The spider then guided the group in imagining what it would be like for the Spirit of the Earth to be healthy. Her rivers, lakes, and oceans clean. Her forests green and tall. Her air pure, fresh, and pristine. Her whole world treated with love and respect.

At that moment, as if the planet had heard their prayers, the earth shook, fire from a volcano exploded into the sea, and a rainbow appeared across the sky!

Lil Gorilla jumped up. "It's a message for us! How about we call the festival PACHA JAMMA in honor of Pachamama!"

The rest of the group agreed. "Let's do this!" they shouted.

CHAPTER 7

TELL THE WORLD

But as Pacha soon found out, it's easier talking about doing something than actually doing it. Especially when no one had ever done anything like throw the biggest festival ever. Naming the event "PACHA JAMMA" seemed like the only thing they all could agree on. There was so much to do and yet everyone had different ideas of what should be done.

Jag wanted famous leaders and presidents to speak about the climate. Pebble wanted rock & roll music. Señor imagined connecting all the networks, so all species could share stories. Wilder wanted the festival to be broadcast to all the rivers and oceans worldwide, following the flow of natural water cycles. Hum hoped the Main Stage would highlight the "endangered species" to make sure their gifts wouldn't be lost forever. Tree wanted extra attention on sharing ideas about what to do with the problems of the world. The little platypus just wanted to sing and rap! And Pacha noticed that every time they almost agreed on an idea, Mr. Tick would start an argument about why it was stupid.

Finally, Pacha stomped her feet and drew some dusty lines on the ground with her big toe. "Let's just have the stages divided by natural borders—like where the polar tundra meets the forests or where the tropics meets the desert—so that everyone can have their special area and not keep fighting about things that don't matter to them!"

"I love it!" Señor chimed in. "These natural areas are like habitats and each of them can have a stage to host 'teams' who solve the problems of their world. It'll be like that crazy insect festival called Burning Mantis—but without all the crazies!"

Still though, they needed someone to be in charge of these "Action Stages." Someone needed to make sure everything was running on time with the solar or lunar clocks. This was obviously a hard job.

Pacha was feeling a little itchy and concerned under her gorilla mask. She realized that if everyone didn't have a role to play, they'd all keep stepping on each other's toes. This whole idea about who should be in charge of the Action Stages was no different. Nobody wanted to do it! Well, except for Mr. Tick, who seemed eager to be in charge wherever he wasn't wanted.

"This festival is missing something that I can help with," he said. "There are lots of starving creatures that would love to come and make merriment. Like, for example, my parasite brothers. No one has even thought of them! Maybe we pair each of them with a mammal for food, traveling, or dancing on? I say this because if we don't make things right for the parasites, we'll surely have a mutiny! And I wouldn't want to see a species war destroy your little love fest because of a simple error..."

Jag clenched his jaw and shook his head. Hum's chest puffed up angrily and Tree bristled her leaves in annoyance. Pacha was frustrated by these crazy threats from an insect who looked uglier than an earwig after a sleepless night. "*Anyway*," she said, rolling her eyes. "Can we talk about how we're getting the word out? We have a giant event to produce, not a paradise for parasites."

Pacha wasn't exactly volunteering though. She didn't really want to chase a bunch of crazy animals to a party nor did she want to have anything to do with the Action Stages! She worried that she might bumble her words or forget her message while she was on stage. And if anyone found out she was a human, they might feed her to the crocodiles. She thought the "truce" might not apply to humans.

Thankfully, most of the others were excited to get the word out about PACHA JAMMA to their "families" even though they knew it would be difficult, if not dangerous.

Though Pacha was not thrilled about "getting the word out"—she felt handicapped by her lack of experience in the wild—she wanted to do her part. She was asked to tell all the primates, of course. She just hoped that she wouldn't mess up. Unfortunately, her worries came true the night before she was to leave, when she found herself coughing and sneezing like she was in a hay field. She told Señor that she wasn't sure if she was the right gorilla for the job.

"Don't worry!" Señor said. "We're all kind of like the moon—we have our shadow sides. But don't let what you can't see spook you or stop you. Being a hero is about being scared and doing it anyway!"

The next morning, everyone agreed on some basic rules. First off, leave no trace. Shortcuts are okay, if no one gets hurt. Speciesism is not cool. Honesty is mandatory. In the final huddle before they left, they each put a hand, paw, flipper, wing, or branch together. Looking each other in the eyes, everyone shouted together *"Vamonos!"* and zoomed off in different directions like snowflakes in a blizzard.

Pacha watched as Pebble rocked and rolled the news to the mountaintops and down to the valleys. Tree branched out and gave invitations far and wide, even working with her apple friends to send tree-mails through the farms. Hum spread the word to all of the flowers. Whale made a million calls with her beautiful ocean songs. Señor had fun telling the fungi. The spiders spun instant messages across the world wide web. MC Plat the platypus sang his watery way throughout the river paths. And finally, after spitting on her PJs with frustration, Mr. Tick jumped off Pacha's shoulder, scurrying off into the forest. She was thrilled to get rid of that annoying bug, at least for a little while.

Pacha took a deep breath. With PACHA JAMMA leaflets in a satchel across her chest, she started down a trail. Though she knew she had to reach all the continents to tell the primate world, she had no idea how to get there. Still, she hoped to reach at least ten monkey meteorologists, nine bonobo builders, eight orangutan engineers, seven tarsier technicians, six lemur librarians, five bushbaby bankers, four marmoset midwives, three ape architects, two gorilla gardeners, and one handy howler.

Pacha felt she had set out on the next leg of an epic adventure. At first she thought she could skip across the whole world! But skipping got old really soon. And walking felt like she was a tortoise in deep sand. Recalling how quickly the others zoomed off, she felt discouraged, knowing that she might be wandering for months like a gypsy with no caravan. "Why me?!" she asked herself.

"Would you like a ride?" a voice called out. Lil Gorilla looked over to see a beautiful black horse. She smiled and hopped on. The horse's name was Buster, a friendly stallion. He explained how he had trotted off from his home at the stables when a gate was accidentally left open. A week had passed and Buster was having a hard time being free. "Once you get out, what does one do? I don't know where my family is, and all my friends are still racing or jumping. I've heard that there are wild horses and great things in the world to see, but I would love someone to experience it with!"

SONG LYRICS—HORSES DON'T SEE COLORS (LIKE PEOPLE DO)

VERSE 1

Buster is this horse I know
His coat is smooth and black
He's got two socks as white as snow
And he's real proud of that
He dances and he prances
with a saddle on his back
And he told me you might want to know
this special little fact

CHORUS

Horses don't see colors
The same way people do
We just love each other
Red, black, white, or blue
We know a horse is still a horse
So he told me to tell you
Horses don't see colors
The same way people do

VERSE 2

When Buster runs through the fields
All his friends come 'round
They toss their tails and click their heels,
they make quite a sound
There's big ol' Red and Jack the Gray

A white horse and a brown
They run and jump as they play
Better friends can't be found

CHORUS

Horses don't see colors
The same way people do
We just love each other
Red, black, white, or blue
We know a horse is still a horse
So he told me to tell you
Horses don't see colors
The same way people do

VERSE 3

Buster said to tell you
When you're making friends
Make them in all colors
And you'll be just like them
And they have so much fun
So I hope you will agree
That we should love all colors
Just like Buster said to me

CHORUS

Horses don't see colors
The same way people do
We just love each other
Red, black, white, or blue
We know a horse is still a horse

So he told me to tell you
Horses don't see colors
The same way people do
                    Lyrics by Jackie Carlyle

Buster whinnied and set off at a canter. As Pacha's excitement grew, she noticed that the more she trusted Buster, the more he trusted her. Soon they were in perfect harmony and it seemed as though Buster knew where to go naturally. "A friendship based on trust can make miracles!" the wise horse said.

Soon, they were moving at warp speed, even passing trains and sports cars. As the stallion galloped from urban jungles to vast and dense forests, Lil Gorilla gave PACHA JAMMA invitations to the presidents, kings, and queens of every primate nation. All in all, she told 543 species, 72 genera, and 13 different families!

CHAPTER 8

GREATNESS IS HARD WORK

When Lil Gorilla and Buster returned to the festival location, they shared their best stories around the fire, including how they eluded some poachers in the Congo.

The next morning, Jag rose on his hind legs to open the meeting. "Thank you all for your dedication to getting the word out! It looks like it's working, as we've heard from thousands of species around the world that they're coming to the party! There's just a few things to work out. First of all, who is going to be in charge of these Action Stages." Jag stroked his beard. "I propose that we have a secret vote to see who gets the job." He chuckled as he handed out voting cards.

Before they voted, each of the others, including Pacha, gave a short speech about why they would NOT be good for the job. (Except Mr. Tick, of course.)

Nevertheless, when all cards were counted, every vote except two was for Lil Gorilla. Pacha didn't understand why she would have been chosen, having explained that she had so little experience and didn't like speaking in groups. But she hesitantly accepted the role of Action Stage Leader anyway. Everyone, except for Mr. you-know-who, applauded Lil Gorilla for her bravery and willingness to take on this important job.

"If I don't do it, I'll be like one of those primates who only thinks of themselves while the world is crying for help...your problem is my problem."

Changing the subject, Jag said that they still needed to figure out who would perform on the Main Stage, besides Pebble's rock star friends. Wilder spouted and said that all species should get at least 15 seconds of fame and that performances could be in any style. Hum zipped about excitedly, suggesting they go 24 hours a day, so that the nocturnal creatures would feel welcome too. Champignón popped up

with another great idea, saying that the whole festival should be about CHANGE! Everyone loved that idea, except for the genetically modified corn and soybeans that had recently taken root in the area. They had already changed enough.

Peering through bamboo binoculars, Pacha could see that the festival grounds were actually connecting all the different biomes of the world. From the tropics to the mountainous snow to the ocean blue, every climate and species could survive in this diverse wonderland. Already, she saw campers arriving, mainly bugs marching into the insect quarters or camels carrying things. The fleas were setting up a market for exchanging supplies and selling food.

Hum held a contest to design the stadium and many teams submitted ideas. The marine mammals and the amphibians wanted the stadium to be an enormous underground crystal cave. The cats wanted it to be shaped like a giant milk bowl. Tree suggested they skip the risky

stadium idea and just put the performances in a redwood grove. But an osprey assisted by a magpie and a robin had the winning design—a ginormous BIRD'S NEST!

Looking at the plans, Lil Gorilla and Hum once again realized how large a project this really was. In the wind, they sent word for volunteers to help with the building. Pebble gathered huge dump-loads of sand and the bedrock for the foundation to the stadium. Tree and her cousins donated massive branches. Señor helped everyone find a task and gave pep talks whenever they got tired. When the Spider named Auntie Sage put the word out for builders, gazillions of ants, termites, birds, beavers, and spiders showed up.

Species helped ship and deliver the equipment for the stadium. The fireflies put up the lighting. The sunflowers captured sunlight and turned

it into electricity for the stadium and the Action Stages. The beavers built dams with turbines and windmills to power the lights when the sun was not shining. The Electric Eel Company charged backup batteries with energy from the tides. Everyone worked long hours to get the stadium ready for opening day. The stage was half-land, half-water. Sun lit the stage by day, and Moon by night.

Meanwhile, questions still circulated across the ocean news channels: Will Pacha Jamma solve all the problems of the world?

Slithering,

  whistling,

    popping,

      rocking...

Will these wild animals get everything done in time?

Rolling,

  roaring,

    beating,

      shaking...

Will anyone even come?

Squawking,

  crinkling,

    locking,

      mooing...

Wing by wing, hoof by hoof, leaf by leaf... everyone came! The turtles, snails, and slugs were the last to arrive—late as usual. The entire planet came—except for the humans. Pacha was so thrilled, she felt like she had butterflies in her stomach. Suddenly butterflies flew over the stage, painting the sky with their colorful wings. With that, finally, opening day had come and the show was ready to begin!

"YEEEEEEAAAAAAAA!!!"

CHAPTER 9

WELCOME TO PACHA JAMMA!

T he wild crowd went wilder as Wilder the Whale spouted her greeting from the underwater stage: "Welcome to PACHA JAMMA, the greatest earth festival ever! We're in tough times...we need to come together to change the tide! When we're all connected, we can halt the destruction of our home. So, just to show everyone that we're serious about changing the future, let's make the biggest wave ever!"

Jag leapt onto the stage and led the crowd in a massive wave around the roaring stadium. The fierce cat smiled bigger than Pacha had ever seen. He jumped forward, stepping out of his seriousness for a second, howling to the audience:

"We are here to laugh, boogie, and become friends with all of our relations! The performers are as old as four billion years and as young as

FUN FACT

How do you relate to your relations?

When peoples of the world pray and speak of "All My Relations" (for instance, "Mitayuke Oyasin" in the Lakota language), we are talking not only about our human relatives, but also the spirits of plants, rocks, animals, and even natural forces. How would your relationship with the world around you be transformed if you saw all things as your mother, father, brother, sister, or even yourself? What if you knew that all things that live are supporting one another? This is what Dr. Martin Luther King Jr. meant when he said, "Before you finish eating breakfast this morning, you've depended on more than half the world." In other words, each bite we eat, each item of clothing we wear, each breath we take is a gift from our relations.

• •

a single day. Please enjoy the music and messages from all of the plants, animals, and other creatures! From near and far, across the seven seas, braving fiery deserts, storms and famine...over the mountains, through the woods, and even past grandma's house...we have arrived!"

Lil Gorilla couldn't believe her eyes. There were so many wondrous sights and sounds...

A dolphin breakdancing...
Termites and woodpeckers playing mouth-drums...
A circus of sole fish flipping across the waters...
An octopus singing octaves and mixing eight songs at once...
A duck-billed platypus stage diving...
Bananas going BANANAS...
A black-eyed pea doing a funky dance...
And a beaver named Justin Time was singing too...

Wilder spouted water on Lil Gorilla while announcing the next act:

"Without further ado...everyone...please join the amazing rapper, MC Plat, our choir of coral reefs, and a live Lotus Band in singing 'Welcome to PACHA JAMMA!'" As Pacha shuffled in place, rehearsing her speech in her head, she laughed about this little platypus spinning on his beak.

SONG LYRICS—WELCOME TO PACHA JAMMA

VERSE 1

The greatest show
With amazing flow
Arranged to blow
With the wind and the crow
With your paws and leafs
Just let 'em grow
Like the laws of nature
It's a rock rock star...
A parade of parrots...
A rainbow's light show...
An insect band named the Beetles...
All you need is love
Dreams and peace
Just like the dove
So raise your paws up
For Mama Earth

CHORUS

Come on and raise your paws
for Mama Earth
It's a dream
Pacha's Pajamas
Come on and let's unite
For Mama Earth
It's a dream
Pacha's Pajamas
Welcome to
the Nature Festival
Pacha Jamma,
Pacha Jamma
It's a dream of
A planet dance for all
Tell your papa
Tell your mama

VERSE 2

Have you ever wondered
How wonderful our world?
How a butterfly flaps
And the wind changes?
Word to your mother
Life ranges
From a lizard to a raven,
A song for all species
All you need is love
Dreams and peace
Just like the dove
So raise your paws up
For Mama Earth

CHORUS

Come on and raise your paws
for Mama Earth
It's a dream
Pacha's Pajamas
Come on and let's unite
For Mama Earth
It's a dream
Pacha's Pajamas
Welcome to...
Nature Festival
Pacha Jamma,
Pacha Jamma
It's a dream of a
planet dance for all
Tell your papa
Tell your mama

BRIDGE

Can you imagine if real foxes were on the news?
If you could hear the ocean sing the blues?
If the chorus to this song was corral reefs?
If 18 carrots went platinum with gold teeth?
If the spiders created the internet?
Or the termites rewrote the hymns of Lent?
What passport for the timberland?
Who's muddy waters to bloom a lotus?
The greatest book was a tree we quoted
Time to resurrect the natural
Like a black-eyed pea it's a rapping call
Where's the love ya'll?
Come on and raise your paws
For Mama Earth

CHORUS

Come on and raise your paws

for Mama Earth

It's a dream

Pacha's Pajamas

Come on and let's unite

For Mama Earth

It's a dream

Pacha's Pajamas

Lyrics by Aaron Ableman

After the welcome song, Jag introduced Lil Gorilla as the host of the Action Stages. This was the moment that Pacha had feared. She would be so embarrassed if the audience didn't like her. But her PJs shimmied her body forward, walking her on stage like a bee drunk on honey. The stadium was glittering with a billion rainbow-colored lights and creatures swaying into the distance. At that moment, time seemed to stand still as she took in the sheer magic that surrounded her.

The water-world of oceans and rivers splashed out in all directions to her right while the terrestrial world of mountains and plains drifted off to her left like a giant Zen painting. All seven domains of animals were present—the reptiles, avians, mammals, and insects on her stage left and the mollusk, arthropod, and chordate domains on her stage right.

The fungus and plant kingdoms were so vast and beautiful that it boggled Pacha's brain. The stadium was a patchwork of species groups, all bunched together in their micro-habitats. Giant ice-sculptures formed the stands for where the penguins, polar bears slid around. Tens of thousands of species of ferns, lichen, and moss squealed like teenagers seeing their favorite pop stary!

Pacha saw turquoise waterfalls lit up with phosphorescent dancers, turning the freshwater streams to glittery disco-ball bubble parties! She marveled at how blue-green algae, wild sponges, and phytoplankton were hugging anchovy and sardine fishes, all taking a week off from eating their favorite aquatic salads. Majestic wildflower fields formed terrestrial bleachers in the stadium hilltops. When the wind picked up, thousands of coconut trees tossed watery refreshments across the stadium!

A giant stand of bamboo swayed in perfect harmony with a humungous underwater seaweed forest. Hundreds of flocks of colorful macaws, flamencos, and hummingbirds, swooped and hovered in midair above center stage. A tomato patch rooted at the base of the stadium bleachers stood ready to jump on stage if anyone had a bad performance! Even creatures Pacha used to be scared of, like the giant squid or anacondas, were being peaceful in this moment!

SONG LYRICS—NATURE SUPERHERO

Where all my Nature Superheroes at?

CHORUS

Nature, Nature in me
Everything I touch
It turns, it turns into me
Everything I hear
My favorite song on repeat
When I hear myself
The world comes clappin' for me
Everybody's Nature is to be free

VERSE 1

Underneath the skin
Inside these bones
Flowing through my blood
And in all through this microphone
To the air to the wind
To the heart of the planet
That lives inside your dome
To the ways of the crowd waving out loud
Cuz it's amazing to be home
It's my nature it's my song
Get wild get down get along
Get up you know what time it is,
It's time in every zone

Yeah we throwin' space parties
Playin' planet music
Slappin' the solar system movin'
Organized through orbits cruising
Naturally, we're never losing

VERSE 2

Pick a star any star
I'll wish it and it tells me who I are
I am my own nature
I'm closer than my breath
I'm better than the best
I got my golden ticket
Oh yeah, oh yeah, oh yes
I'm brighter than sunsets
Rising in the east
Flyer than the bees
Mightier than the trees
There ain't no stoppin' rocking
I'm freezin
I'm rocking beats
They see me knockin' knees
A sleep walking dream
Into a natural thing

CHORUS

Nature, Nature in me
Everything I touch
It turns, it turns into me
Everything I hear
My favorite song on repeat

When I hear myself
The world comes clappin' for me
Everybody's Nature is to be free

VERSE 3

I'm a upside rainbow
Rights side up eggs toast
Richer than your banks
I got my imagination
Crowned in coronation
Voting for my nature
Human like MJ
The Super hero gamer
Toppling all the gangsters
Sunnier than the paints glow
Out up on my Range Ro
Floating streams of change flow
This day I make known
My Nature is so beautiful
My Nature is so beautiful
My Nature is so beautiful

VERSE 4

Living in the eye of that beholder
That just a drop of that sea is close
When we see that we is supposed to
Live as family, Come toast up
One, yes, we are one yes
Let's have some fun, yes
And we have come yes
To piece the world together

Don't puzzle that much
All it takes is nature's touch
Let your love, live and be unhushed
Now's the time but there's no rush
Now's the but there's no rush
Now's the time, but there's no rush
Now's the time, now's the time, now's the time
Come on give it up

CHORUS

Nature, Nature in me
Everything I touch
Il turns, it turns into me
Everything I hear
My favorite song on repeat
When I hear myself
The world comes clappin' for me
Everybody's Nature is to be free
Lyrics by Aaron Ableman and Amani Carey-Simms

Being on Main Stage was a growth moment for Pacha, beautiful and scary at the same time. But surprising herself, she took a deep breath and eagerly accepted the mic.

"Lemme hear you all...go wild!"

The audience roared in their own strange languages. Pacha wasn't sure if they were happy or just crazy, but she kept going anyway:

"Gorillas in the house! Let me hear the big cats! Where my dogs at? What does the fox say? Oh, and if you're a bird, remember to tweet #PACHAJAMMA!

"Thank you all for coming!" Lil Gorilla continued. "I know many of you came a long way to hear some of your favorite music, but PACHA

JAMMA is much more than that! Our planet earth is no longer safe and many of us feel scared, in danger, even angry sometimes."

She paused and let her words sink in. "Maybe PACHA JAMMA is a way to change many of our problems at once?!"

"Can you shut up already and get the party started!" a troublemaker in the crowd yelled.

When the heckler quieted down, Lil Gorilla bravely continued, explaining the Action Stages and teams. She invited everyone to visit the stage of their home habitats and to join an action team. The crowd still responded with much less enthusiasm than she had hoped for.

Suddenly feeling awkward, she tripped up on her final words and accidently snorted like a hog!

This angered a wild pig, who rushed the stage through the giraffe-guards' long legs. He came towards the Lil Gorilla, tossing his head and oinking at her for dishonoring his species! Lil Gorilla jumped away from the wild pig while the audience chuckled nervously, hoping the entire

scene was a bad joke. As the cameras flashed, Lil Gorilla ran off stage, feeling humiliated.

Pacha found a tidal pool to relax in and figure out her next moves. Floating on her back in the warm seawater, she rehashed what had just happened over and over in her mind. She regretted not standing up for herself. Never again, she told herself.

Suddenly, a giant shark fin rose out of the water! Scared, Pacha scrambled onto a rock on the shore. As the fin got closer, she started panicking before remembering that just makes things worse. A smiling shark surfaced with a plastic soda bottle on his tongue. He nudged the bottle toward Lil Gorilla and explained that he had found it in an ocean current on his way to the show. He also told her, for future reference, that sharks don't even like the taste of primates! Not knowing what else to do, she smiled and grabbed the bottle. And with that, the shark waved a fin at her and swam away.

Sure enough, there was a message in the bottle! She twisted off the cap, and used a stick to fish out a piece of parchment paper. The message looked to be gibberish words around images of a cat, two sheep—each with funny symbols or signs next to them—and a shaggy mammal she did not recognize. For some reason, the mysterious message gave Pacha a weird feeling.

CHAPTER 10

MESSAGE IN A BOTTLE

P acha rushed toward the Main Stage to find her friends. She found
Hum in a "Nesting & Resting" area behind the dressing rooms.
Sitting in the grass to catch her breath, Pacha told the bird about
the message the shark intercepted.

"*Nena*, Mr. Tick's prints are all over this!" Hum said after contemplating
the news. "If anyone was going to mess with PACHA JAMMA, what part
of the festival would they target?"

She and Pacha looked at each for a moment and simultaneously
both yelled "The Action Stages!" They set off for the massive Apple Tree
that hosted PACHA JAMMA's broadcasting station so they could monitor
all the Action Stages at once.

As Lil Gorilla hustled to keep up with Hum, she muttered "Not on my watch!" Arriving at the Apple Tree, Lil Gorilla and Hum watched Tree-V monitors for unusual activities at the different stages.

On the River Stage, a group of amphibians were just settling into a talk sponsored by the indicator species team featuring the director of the Hop-On-It Frog Choir, Ms. Abbey Toad. On the Forest Stage, Poison Ivy was leading the other forest guardians through a workshop on the need to limit human activities in nature and ways to stop the wrecking of the wild. On other stages, they saw plants and animals enjoying icebreakers like musical chairs, laughing yoga, and tai chi.

Pacha suggested that Señor might have some ideas. They found him in the roots below, running the Interspecies Internet while helping a hackathon make apps to improve cross-species teamwork. Like a mad scientist, Señor was connecting roots and helping them grow. He was also working with popular spider websites to get the message out about what was happening at #PACHAJAMMA. Birds were tweeting in the branches above. Insects were posting and apples were computing all the information. PACHA JAMMA was going viral!

Upon hearing Lil Gorilla's news, a visibly disturbed Señor pulled up a series of charts showing what was happening on all the different online networks. As with any huge collection of data, it was hard to see patterns at the beginning. But Señor just kept flipping through the charts until he saw something.

One of the charts showed an alarming growth of activity on the Parasites Network over the past several weeks. "I knew it!" Hum said. "What is that crazy tick up to?"

Señor called over the captain of the underground team—a nearsighted mole named Revere, and asked her to focus the entire team on hacking into Mr. Tick's computer system. Revere scampered off with her rodent buddies into the root tunnels where they might tap into the parasite network.

After about an hour, Revere returned. Mr. Tick's computer had strong security and they would need days, if not weeks, to break in. "But we don't have days or weeks," Pacha murmured, lost in thought. Then she offhandedly asked Revere what she made of the symbols next to the sheep on the message.

Revere couldn't place the symbols but thought they looked human, so she opened up a wormhole to the Internet. "Symbols are one of the most powerful ways that humans understand each other," said the mole. "I've been seeing a lot of animal and plant networks adopt them, especially the emoji."

Revere dragged the two icons to the Image search bar and both times the search showed many versions of a single circle drawn around both symbols. "Let's see! It's called a Yin and Yang...it's about how opposite forces are actually interconnected and in balance. Yin is associated with the negative, the feminine, and the moon while yang is associated with the positive, the masculine, and the sun!"

Suddenly Pacha remembered a school trip to a local farm. She figured that the Yang sheep must be a ram while the Yin sheep must be a ewe!

Now all they had to do was figure out the last animal in the message. The team decided that Señor would monitor the grasslands and savannah biome stages for the mystery animal. Revere and her team would see what they could find on the biome networks. Hum would do flyovers of the different stages. And Lil Gorilla would find Jag who—as head of the Organization of Organized Organisms—would almost certainly be able to help her identify the final animal.

She found the big cat taking a break from the stadium in a grassy meadow. Jag rubbed his furry chin as Lil Gorilla told him about the message in the bottle, a cat, a Yang ram, a Yin ewe, and Mr. Tick's computer. He didn't perk up until she rolled out the message.

"That's a wildebeest! I saw one at the Savannah Stage. They might still be there. Gotta go!" Jag then bounded off, rushing back to the Main Stage to officiate the Nature Superhero contest.

Even though Pacha now knew all the animals, she was at a loss for what to do.

She found herself strolling off into the forest, remembering that her papa had said that taking a walk helps you think clearly. But after a thousand steps, she felt no closer to solving the puzzle. As she walked she hardly noticed that the trees and brush were actively clearing a path for her. And before she knew it, she was standing in front of Tree, who was swaying in the wind.

Tree opened her eyes and whispered, "if walking is not working, perhaps mindfulness or stretching could be the answer." Tree then stretched her branches wide and tall, guiding Lil Gorilla through several different yoga poses. On the final pose, Pacha had an inspiration—perhaps every animal image on the message could be replaced with the name of the animal!

Despite still being unable to read the message, Pacha had a feeling that she was on the right track. Just then, she thought about PACHA JAMMA! She had to get back to her duties at the stages.

CHAPTER 11

LAY OF THE LAND

O ver the next two days, Lil Gorilla visited all the stages across the different habitats and visited dozens of action teams working on different issues.

On a dock at the Ocean Stage, she met with the Oil Spill Response team, which included whales, dolphins, otters, and oyster mushrooms. When she met with the overfishing and ocean plastic teams, she was introduced to a clownfish and a mermaid, who chuckled about how popular their species had become in human movies! On the Savannah Stage, she visited the Disappearing Team, full of lions, rhinos, gorillas, and other victims of poaching. On the Tundra Stage, she met with the glacier tracking team of caribou and huskies, who talked about how the world's weather is changing.

At the Forest Stage, she met with the reforestation team. While she was hanging out and listening to stories, an awesome migration of butterflies arrived. One butterfly even rapped the story of his life cycle, sharing the hope that we can all emerge from our own chrysalis and fly away free.

SONG LYRICS—BUTTERFLY LIFE

You know butterflies love pianos
We go together like...

VERSE 1

Let me break it down,
Make it plain
Tell you cut and dry
How I get by

Living the life of a butterfly
Nature's OG
I'm a pollen transporter
They call me OT
Original transformer
Cuz I used to be a caterpillar
Till I metamorphized
Used to have 16 legs
And six pair of eyes
I spent my free time
Dreaming about the sky
I was stuck on the ground wishing I could fly
My only job was to grub
I wipe my plate clean
Living the life of a vegan
Eating them leafy greens
The flowers bloom
I'm breaking out of cocoons
Artists are inspired by
I'm making them swoon
But now I put my larvae days behind me
Flying through the air
Is where you'll find me
When I was a caterpillar
Yeah I got grimy
Now I take flight
And it's way more exciting

CHORUS

Fly fly away, sing out for your light
Fly fly away, sing out for your light

Fly fly away, sing out for your light
Fly fly away, sing out for your light

VERSE 2

It's that butterfly life
The moth is my cousin
And sometimes we fly alike
As I fly flutter by
Like a thought running through your mind
I'm proud of my species
We got many different kinds
We got moth-butterflies
True butterflies and skippers
Watch you plant flowers in your garden
And I kiss 'em
If nature is a painter
And our canvas is blank
Then we callin' it the forest
And my colors is the paint
My caterpillars days are still a part of me
Whole kingdoms are named after me
They callin' it a monarchy
I'm a great subject for photography
In the park
Little kids follow me
Like the pied piper
Except it ain't the music
It's the colors
Butterfly life you gotta love it
Except it ain't the music
It's the colors
Butterfly life you gotta love it

CHORUS

Fly fly away, sing out for your light

Fly fly away, sing out for your light

Lyrics by Talib Kweli and Aaron Ableman

To make things even more awesome, a group of bubbly bear cubs sang a song calling for everyone to wake up! They were with their papa, a famous singing bear from the 1960s. Papa Bear's voice was scratchy like something you'd hear on an old record player.

SONG LYRICS—WAKE UP EVERYBODY

CHORUS

We've got to change the world

Got to make it better

We've got to change the world

Got to make it better

We've got to change the world

VERSE 1

Wake up everybody
No mo' hibernatin'
Open up your eyes
Wipe that sleepy ol' sand
The world has changed so very much
From what it used to be
So many dying bumblebees

CHORUS

We've got to change the world
We've got to make it better
We've got to change the world
We've got to make it better
We've got to change the world

VERSE 2

Wake up all the teachers
Time to teach a new way
Maybe then they'll listen
To whatcha have to say
Cause they're the ones who's coming up
The world is in their paws
When you teach the young'uns
Teach 'em the very best you can
The world won't get no better if we just let it be
The world won't get no better we gotta change it
You and me.
We've got to change the world
Got to make it better

VERSE 3

Wake up all the players
Time to play a new game
When you're gone
Watcha want them to say
They was all about
Making a better place
I know we can do it
If we all say our grace
The world won't get no better if we just let it be
The world won't get no better we gotta change it
You and me.

VERSE 4

Wake up all the dreamers
Time to dream a new dream
And this one ain't about you or me
Let's build a foundation
For the castles in the sky
What we put in our wings
Together we will fly
The world won't get no better if we just let it be
The world won't get no better we gotta change it
You and me.

CHORUS

We've got to change the world
Got to make it better
We've got to change the world
Got to make it better
We've got to change the world

Lyrics by Dave Room and Aaron Ableman based on the original lyrics by
John Whitehead, Gene McFadden and Victor Carstarphen.

Unfortunately, the song caused a bit of a controversy, as a group of chipmunks and squirrels sleeping in their burrows didn't want to wake up from hibernation quite yet. Just then, a gang of parasites with megaphones rose up from the back of Papa Bear's fur. They heckled the bears, saying that their message of planetary awakening was impossible. Lil Gorilla asked them to please "Be Respectful!" or she'd call for the trees to sweep them out of the forest. Though they kept quiet from then on, Pacha worried that they'd be up to something else soon.

After Lil Gorilla ran off for the River Stage, she met with the indicator species, water impurity, and dam teams. They told her that contaminated water kills more humans every year than all of their wars combined. "I can only imagine what this dirty water does to plants and animals!" she thought to herself. At the Grassland Stage, she met with the Pollinator

Team, which was actually putting on a special fashion show for the wildflowers and roses. *Que linda!*

At the Alpine Stage, Pacha got a little light-headed from so little oxygen in the high altitude. She stumbled off to the Cultivated Lands Stage, where they got riled up about air pollution, water contamination, soil contamination, genetic engineering, and global warming. "There's NO I IN TEAM!" a honeybee yelled, angry about how disorganized everything had become. At the Desert Stage, she met with the desertification, mining, and erosion teams where they talked mostly about what steps they would take after the festival was over.

At the Jungle Stage, Pacha met with the Primates for Pachamama Team. She asked if anyone had seen the mysterious wildebeest, but no one seemed to know who that was.

Through her travels among the stages, Pacha got a lay of the land and a much fuller sense of the how large PACHA JAMMA was now that everyone had settled in. The stadium was at the center of the festival grounds where the habitats converged. Each habitat had its own stage surrounded by its own mini-festival run by huge volunteer crews. Here the inhabitants camped, fed themselves, made and traded crafts, got child care, and relaxed.

Pacha quickly discovered that the mini-festivals in the various areas were very different. She felt most at home in the Forest Fair, which was situated in a magical old-growth forest. The great horned owl from the Deforestation Team meeting told her that the forest was preserved by something called a "Land Trust" around the turn of the 20th century. Paths lined with food and craft booths curved through the forest. Stages hosted performances of all types from music to theater to spoken word poetry to improv.

And everywhere Pacha looked there were trees. In all her life, she had never experienced or imagined anything quite like it. It was a kaleidoscope of plants and animals. Nothing stood out because there was something everywhere you looked. Every 100 feet she walked, she'd see something that blew her mind!

Belly dancers, drum circles, sudden parades that anyone could join, fortune tellers, poetry slams, storytellers, vaudeville acts, stilt walkers, and much more. A meadow for young plants and animals had face painting, puppet shows, hula hooping, juggling, circus acts, and other fun stuff to do and see.

Everyone here was respectful, very different from the kids at Pacha's school. In fact, Pacha witnessed some of the most beautiful friendships blossom at the fair. It seemed like everyone knew they were connected to each other and the forest.

Pacha found the food in the Forest Fair like no diner or restaurant she had ever seen. There was chia fudge brownies, almond butter omelets, hempnut cookies, tempeh burgers, spinach apple turnovers, organic kettle corn, kale smoothies, coconut ice cream, and veggie sushi! "Now say that ten times fast!" Pacha thought with a giggle. She discovered that the best booths had the longest lines.

Late at night, once the larger groups were shooed out, the REAL party began. The fair turned into a city of lights and sights. Only fair volunteers, performers, artisans, food vendors, and organizers like Pacha who had ALL PACHA JAMMA passes were allowed to stay.

For the first time since she had been in this strange and

wonderful land, Pacha noticed the stars. They were so much brighter than in the city. Up until now, she hadn't a chance to take a breather or relax. She finally let go and embraced the moment. She could not imagine a better movie than just sitting back and watching the stars form characters and stories in the sky.

A shooting star made her remember the stories her *abuelita* told her about the origin of the universe, and her mama saying that we are all made of stardust... like everything else. Pacha made a wish that she would be able to fully experience her connection with her namesake, Pachamama. Sitting under the stars, Pacha had the sense that everything was living in a natural world order and that PACHA JAMMA was part of its evolution.

But each habitat was totally unique. For example, she got an entirely different feeling at the hot and dry desert habitat, which was more like the festival her father always talked about called Burning Man. Though she still regretted her performance on the Main Stage, she was actually happy with her performance as Action Stage Leader!

CHAPTER 12

MONKEY TRAPS

As she ate breakfast the next day, Pacha thought about the message from the bottle. She whistled for Hum. Hum whizzed over. Pacha told Hum what Jag had said about the wildebeest. Hum said she hadn't seen the mysterious wildebeest but zipped off to take another look.

Minutes later, Hum whizzed back and hovered in front of Pacha. "That wildebeest is headed to the Savannah Stage now but I have to go to the Grasslands Stage for a Pollinators meeting." Knowing that pollinators were big-time gossips, Pacha decided to tag along. Maybe they had picked up some news as they went from flower to flower.

As they approached the stage, the buzzing of the bees and wasps was overwhelming. Pacha remembered the time her mother had to tweeze out the stinger of a bee that Pacha accidently stepped on at the park. Although the sting hurt, she felt more sorry for the bee than anything else. But even though she wasn't really scared of bees, a part of her was deathly afraid of wasps.

As she started to turn back, Hum reminded her that all of nature had signed a truce for the duration of PACHA JAMMA. Pacha was still a little skeptical that the truce extended to humans but Hum assured her that it covered everyone. After all, Hum exclaimed, if not, wouldn't a mountain lion or jaguar have eaten her by now?

During the pollinators meeting, Pacha showed the message to the bees and wasps. They looked at the partially decrypted message with confusion. One bee suggested that Mr. Tick's way of thinking is so backward, and that he really needs to change. At that, Pacha realized that the words in the message might be ... backward!

She then unscrambled the message:

At my mark — jewel wasp attack — eltseebedliwj stage — final night.

One of the wise old woman wasps said that the jewel wasps were a cult of brain-controlling wasps. Pacha was horrified to learn that one sting could turn mammals into zombies. Not good news but at least Pacha had a sense of what they were up against. No one, however, had any idea what the "eltseebedliwj" meant. As Pacha prepared to leave, the pollinator team offered to help out however they could. Pacha and Hum thanked them and set off for the Savannah Stage to find the wildebeest, hoping that it could help solve the last part of the puzzle.

Pacha and Hum arrived at the Savannah Stage just as the wildebeest was leaving. It had been a long day and the wildebeest was ready for some down time. Pacha and Hum told the wildebeest about the message in the bottle, how they had almost cracked the code, and the dead end they found themselves in. The tired wildebeest said it had no idea what "eltseebedliwj" meant. As the wildebeest turned to leave, on a whim, Pacha asked, "Do you have any other names?"

"Yep, that I do—some friends call me gnu."

Pacha almost swallowed her tongue but managed to stammer.

"It's not eltseebedliwj...it's elungj—Jungle! They're going to attack the jungle stage!"

Feeling both triumph and fear, Pacha raced after Hum, who had darted off to the Jungle Stage to warn the primates about the attack. But when she got to the stage, no one was around. Just as they were about to call security, Hum noticed a bunch of bonobos and monkeys high in the branches above watching Tree-V. On the screen was a human girl bravely speaking on behalf of the rocks, trees, and waters at another earth festival!

Lil Gorilla climbed up to the canopy and excitedly blurted out, "I bet there are other kids that want to help nature too." The primates laughed, saying that there would likely be so few, it'd take a miracle to make a difference.

A monkey with a floppy hat and a pipe said that he was not so sure. "A planetary awakening is underway. There will soon be millions, if not billions, of humans ready for our Coming Home to Nature program. We just need a way to reach them with the right message!" He paused and thought for a moment. "Maybe we could connect our primate network to the human Internet."

"I like that idea!" said a lemur wearing a huge pair of sunglasses to protect his sensitive eyes. "If we can meet on the same level as the humans, they'll only know you're a monkey or an ape if you choose to tell them! Using this Internet, through music and stories, we can change the dream of humanity!"

The rest of the primates hooted in a mix of confusion and excitement.

"I don't mean to put a damper on things, but..." Lil Gorilla interrupted. She told them about the wasp attack. The primates hollered and beat their chests, shouting that they were ready to defend themselves and PACHA JAMMA. A chimp suggested considering nonviolence but the others ignored her and continued beating their chests.

Lil Gorilla, however, got their attention when she said one sting from a jewel wasp could turn the most alpha primate into a zombie. She suggested that they form a new action team to stop the attack on the Jungle Stage and asked the primates to lead the recruiting so she could get back to her duties as Action Stage Leader. The primates agreed, Hum flew off, and Pacha scampered towards the Main Stage to give her next update.

As she walked, Pacha felt a raindrop and then another and another. She wondered if a storm might be coming. "Well, we need the rain, right?" she thought. "It could fun, maybe—like frolicking in a water park!" She tried to catch raindrops with her tongue but there weren't enough to satisfy her growing thirst. She needed something refreshing to cool and calm her down.

Pacha found herself looking for coconuts in a nearby grove. She recalled watching her *abuelita* chop the top off of a coconut like a ninja, drinking the coconut water, and then scooping out the meat with a piece of the husk. If only she had her *abuelita*'s machete. Surprisingly, Pacha found what looked like a freshly opened coconut lying on the ground. Upon further inspection, however, she realized that the water was gone and the coconut was tied to a stake.

"Does everything have to be a riddle?!" thought Pacha, annoyed. She was about to drop the coconut when she noticed something shiny inside. She thrust her hand in the hole to grab the shiny thing, but try as she might, she couldn't wrangle it out.

Pacha looked up and saw dozens of chubby ticks slowly rappelling toward her on tiny rope ladders. She knew that they meant no good. But she couldn't bear to let go of the shiny thing. She felt a weird twist in her tummy. Not really a bad feeling, but it didn't feel good either.

As if coming out of a fog, she felt the arm of her PJs pressing on her inner wrist, which made her want to let go. Pacha was confused. She felt a new sense of danger as her hand began to hurt and her breath

grew short. For some reason she really wanted the shiny thing, but she trusted her PJs. When she accepted that she wasn't going to have the shiny thing, her belly felt better! Pacha dropped the coconut and stepped away just as a pile of ticks fell directly on the coconut. As they screamed in frustration, Pacha shook her head, stuck out her tongue, and hightailed away.

CHAPTER 13

THE STORM

Pacha made her way back to the Main Stage at the stadium in time to see some komodo dragons perform. Shortly after she arrived, however, it started raining cats and dogs. Not real cats and dogs, of course, just tons of rain showering down.

At first, many of the savanna and grasslands dwellers cheered, as they had been in a long drought. But as the storm picked up momentum, murmurs of worry traveled across the stadium. Like dominos, the frogs sounded an alarm across the stadium: "Ribbit change climate change ribbit change climate change ribbit!"

A windstorm blew in like a wild goblin. Screeching through the crowds, the wind knocked out one of the largest stadium lights, sending the moths into a frenzy. The security "o-fish-als" sounded an alarm that the tide was rising quickly. By then, everyone was running for cover.

Mothers comforted their babies as they dove underground, swam underwater, squeezed inside tree bark, or huddled into buffalo circles.

After the wind died down and everyone returned to the stadium, the loudspeakers blared a public service message—the PACHA JAMMA festival was in the eye of the hurricane!

Everything went totally silent and calm. Sadly, that moment lasted only a moment. A huge lightning bolt lit up the sky, followed almost immediately by a monstrous thunderclap and a blinding downpour.

Frantic animals stampeded for the exits. Hum whizzed up to Pacha. "Follow me or you'll get crushed!" she yelled.

FAUX NEWS
LIVE
PACHA JAMMA IN EYE OF HURRICANE

Lil Gorilla raced behind the bird, dipping and bobbing through the crowd. Following Hum's lead, she barely managed to grab hold of a thrashing branch from a large olive tree. Pulling herself up, she could see a river of animals being swept down toward the ocean waves crashing against the stadium seating.

"That tree's not safe to be in with all this wind and lightning. Let's go!" Hum urged, and Lil Gorilla reluctantly climbed back down. When they finally made their way out of the stadium, they ran into Papa Bear and his grand-cubs. Lil Gorilla worried that the cute little cubs could

get hurt in the storm. She asked Papa Bear whether he had a safe place for them to spend the night. He nodded and said they were headed to his old hibernating grounds—the caves in the mountains between the temperate forest and the tundra.

Lil Gorilla rounded up some friends and they all set off. Following the old bear's lead, Lil Gorilla, Hum, MC Plat, Jag, and a friendly cobra marched into the mountains to find cover for the night. They were lucky that no one got hurt, considering that they were scrambling up muddy mountain goat trails in the middle of the night, with rain pounding down on them.

When they arrived at the cave, they took a moment of silence to give thanks for their good fortune. The space was larger than the theater at Pacha's school. She noticed that the cave had three openings leading deeper into the mountain. The thought of exploring them filled her with curiosity. But getting some rest was a priority.

Lil Gorilla and the others built leafy beds and settled down for the night. In short order, many of animals drifted off to sleep. The cave echoed with the cubs' snores! Unable to sleep, Lil Gorilla was contemplating what to do when Plat waddled over to her and suggested they could find some quiet in one of the tunnels. But which one?

Plat pointed at each tunnel in sequence as he flowed:

Eenie meanie miney moe
Catch a deer tick by the toe
When he hollers, don't let him go
My mama told me be very brave
when you enter a cave!

When he stopped, Plat was pointing at the middle tunnel. They cautiously entered it, Plat leading the way. Lil Gorilla was surprised that she could see anything at all. She hadn't realized that her PJs were glow-in-the-dark. As she trudged through the tunnel, Pacha started thinking about how they were going to get back and wondered out loud if they should mark their trail.

"Let's use what we got," Plat said. "How about...unmmm... rocks?" At each crossroad, they stacked rocks to show where they had come from.

Plat noticed it first—a faint buzzing that grew louder and louder until it was clearly a gathering of mosquitos or wasps. As they crept forward, they heard a sinister cackling, which made Lil Gorilla a little nervous. But when Plat asked if she wanted to turn back, she said no. Soon the tunnel opened up into a large hallway connected to the source of the noise—the boardroom in Mr. Tick's lair!

MC Plat and Pacha crept by a sleeping wasp on the way to the boardroom. Plat hopped onto a small crate so he could see through the window on the door. Inside Mr. Tick was giving a presentation about preventing future PACHA JAMMAs. He showed a map of the entire festival grounds and described how a wasp

attack at the Jungle Stage was the first in a series of attacks that would grow into a species war and ultimately "break this silly truce!" He then presented a slide showing the rise of human population over the past 10,000 years from fewer than ten million to seven billion! He showed

how this mirrored the growth among parasites. In that moment, Pacha realized that Mr. Tick and his minions were trying to keep the world the same for themselves.

She was outraged by their selfishness! And so was Plat, who lost his webbed footing and slipped off the crate, waking up the giant wasp. The guard snarled as he dove toward Lil Gorilla. At the last moment, Plat knocked Lil Gorilla out of the wasp's path. The wasp whizzed past, hit the wall, and slid to the ground. Plat and Lil Gorilla noticed a strange smell emanating from him. "He's releasing pheromones," Lil Gorilla said, recalling a science lesson. "They'll call his brain-controlling wasp friends! We can't stay here!"

As Pacha and Plat sprinted out of Mr. Tick's lair, the buzzing behind them grew louder. At each crossroad they retraced their path thanks to their rock piles, which they dismantled as they ran along. Pacha didn't feel safe until they finally arrived back at the cave with her animal friends. Lil Gorilla gave Plat a hug "good night" and settled into her bed of leaves, no longer bothered by the snoring.

CHAPTER 14

A SONG OF HOPE

B ut Pacha still couldn't sleep. Maybe it was the storm of emotions she was feeling. Disappointed that she hadn't stopped Mr. Tick. Spooked by the dreaded jewel wasps. Unsettled by the destructive weather. Feeling unseen for her true self behind the mask.

She stayed up all night thinking about how to stop the wasps. She remembered what Tree taught her. As she did breathwork, she thought about the how humans have been acting like parasites and parasites like humans because they "never think about anything but themselves and the next day's food." She wondered if that was what was really causing the storm, the problems in nature, and even her health problems. She imagined that humans everywhere might be in a big trap like she had been, grasping for shiny things they don't really need. Pacha thanked herself for staying strong, no matter how tough the journey might be.

Early in the morning, Pacha remembered Mama telling her that that the darkest night is always followed by dawn. With the first light, she went to the mouth of the cave to survey the damage. The storm had destroyed the entire stadium! But rather than regret what had been lost, Pacha focused on seeing PACHA JAMMA rebuilt. After all, she thought, this festival could unite the biosphere and alter the course of the planet.

Out of nowhere, she felt a song in her heart. She began to sing a soft lullaby, feeling the healing energy of the music pulse through her body. A little tree frog joined her, croaking a beautiful melody. Sixteen musical bars later, a couple more frogs and Ms. Abby Toad joined in. Soon a giant orchestra of frogs, toads, and birds was harmonizing across the entire riparian world.

With happiness welling up in her eyes, Pacha watched the clouds part and begin to melt away! Sunlight shone through the retreating

storm clouds, spreading love through the cave, across the festival grounds, and through the biomes! The sound of music brought peace to the land and seas, calming all beings from the smallest to largest.

As the light spread, the animals and plants awakened to a new joy for life. "No matter what, life keeps on living!" thought Pacha, amazed.

Creatures embraced, happy to have survived the storm. The animal, mineral, and vegetable kingdoms honored the moment by bringing a gift of gratitude to an ever-widening circle of beings. Each gift was placed into a mandala honoring those who had fallen in defense of Pachamama. Looking around this giant circle of life, everyone seemed stronger than ever! The natural world had bonded and strengthened as a result of the storm.

Thanks to the dams built by the beavers and meerkats, the major leaks were plugged. Once the stadium area was dry, the ants, bees, termites, and other crafty critters sang work songs as they rebuilt the broken walls, fixed the water damage, and replanted the flower and tree gardens. To help with erosion, millions of seeds popped up from underground, singing "We used to be underground artists but now we're pop stars!"

SONG LYRICS—JUNGLE WORK

CHORUS

Bizzy buzzy
Busy buzzing
jungle work
Bizzy buzzy
jungle work
Ee yai yo
Heave hoe, heave hoe, heave hoe
Ee yai yo ee yai yo

VERSE 1

Even after disaster or a giant crash
No storm can drown our raft
We're together
In any weather that's the task
We float like a hovercraft
Pile one by one like math
Build a farm, build a path
Thru the hills, thru the mountains

When we unite, we can win
Over any trouble or task
The trick of the trade or the top of the class
It's a matter of work, in fact
Oh hammer those nails
Working is so much better when we laugh
Let's just... keep pounding those nails, carrying leaves
Chant, dance like us workin' ants

CHORUS

Bizzy buzzy
Busy buzzing
jungle work
Bizzy buzzy
jungle work
Ee yai yo
Heave hoe, heave hoe, heave hoe
Ee yai yo ee yai yo

VERSE 2

Heidy Hoe Heidy Hoe
It's da termites on a roll
Bringing back this festival
Say yes yes yes yes yes yes ya'll
We use mud, suds, thuds, or soil
Build stadiums and cathedrals
If you only knew, you'd know
We can make dreams grow
Say yes yes ya'll
Raising the roof, heaving and hoeing
with a little bit of... soul

It's off to work, off to work, off to work we go
The way we built new termite city gold
And made a million castles of old ...
Anyone got some wood glue?
I need to fix this catapult

CHORUS

Bizzy buzzy
Busy buzzing
jungle work
Bizzy buzzy
jungle work
Ee yai yo
Heave hoe, heave hoe, heave hoe
Ee yai yo ee yai yo

VERSE 3

Buzzin all around, all around, all around my hours
Unwilting all the flowers
Bazzaz buzzeez bazooz bazours
Bringing sweet to the sour
Dreaming of honey chowder
Giving life an awesome power
Bazzaz buzzeez bazooz bazours
Life is music, make it louder
Strengthen weakened, faith to doubters
The bees make the sad happy all around
Bazzaz buzzeez bazooz bazours
We tell all the flowers that we love them now or
Bazzaz buzzeez bazooz bazours
We'll always be the pride of the hour

Turning the wow into a wowza

CHORUS

Bizzy buzzy
Busy buzzing
jungle work
Bizzy buzzy
jungle work
Ee yai yo
Heave hoe, heave hoe, heave hoe
Ee yai yo ee yai yo

Lyrics by Aaron Ableman

The orangutans, elephants, and hippos partnered to lift up the toppled trees. A giraffe and a crane used their long necks to help put the signs back up while the electric eels repowered the lights.

As the jungle reunited, Lil Gorilla joined the crowds in the mud and muck, cleaning and fixing. It took many long hours, but the hard work finally returned the stadium to its original splendor. Trumpeting elephants announced that the festival was set to resume. Monkeys with air horns called the scaredy-cats back from hiding. Pacha practically floated to the stadium as she saw a herd of baby hippos squealing, "I'm excited, I'm excited..."

Then, for some reason, Pacha thought about what it must be like to be in Mr. Tick's little shoes. Surely, Mr.

Tick seemed very loyal to his parasites. He obviously was trying to make things better for his family. Who could blame him for that? But when it comes at the expense of Pachamama and web of life, Pacha thought "Not here. Not now."

When everyone arrived, there was a feeling that PACHA JAMMA was even stronger than ever. Crowds poured back into the stadium, ready for the fun to resume. Entire classes of animals—like the amphibia, mammalia, and reptilia—were hugging and kissing like a big family reunited!

Lil Gorilla briefed the crowd with the progress of the action teams. She resisted mentioning Mr. Tick's attack because she didn't want to freak them out. Mama would often say "some things are better left unsaid."

She handed off the mic to the beaver Justin Time who brought the stadium to tears with his healing love rap "Water Baby." After that, Sir Elephant wowed the crowd with his spoken word poem about bringing dreams to life.

SONG LYRICS—WATER BABY

INTRO

You're my water baby
You're my water baby
You're my water baby
You're my water baby

VERSE 1

    Boat down the Mississippi
    Motown fish was with me
    Floating with a stick and sticky
    Motions always made me sickly
    Showin' teeth like a grizzly...
    But out of the blue, you saved me
    We rode the tide from the Ganges
    Took a trip across the sand and streams
    Built temples, dance halls, tambourines
    Out of pine trees & our fantasies
    Made music out of our dancing dreams
    Radio me into your underwater taxi
    Gone down but came back free
    I have more lives than a cat, G
    Just in time beaver, that's me
    Even when you miss me, I'll be
    Floating through your memory
    On a boat of wooden mystery
    Just in time love, that's you and me
    Just in time love, that's you and me

PRE CHORUS

    We got love so pure, so true
    It splashes through
    And through and through
    It turns the music to a muse
    Oh makes the river bluer blue

CHORUS

    When I feel your love
    I kiss the river to a sea

You're my water baby

VERSE 2

Sky wish to the blue
Fish to the school
They can't stop you
from loving me now
Can't bite or chomp this down
Prison or junkyard town
Love will save the drowned
Through the ups and down
The ducks and the clowns
Can't lock up these jaws
Dancin' while cupid applauds
Cuz my world is your world
My water is your water, now
My planet is your planet, how
My heart is your heart, wow

PRE CHORUS

We got love so pure, so true
It splashes through
And through and through
It turns the music to a muse
Oh makes the river bluer blue

CHORUS

When I feel your love
I kiss the river to the sea
You're my water baby

Lyrics by Aaron Ableman

Pacha was enjoying the vibes. She was excited to see her friend Señor Champignón come to the stage with a bevy of backup singers. Señor taught the crowd the chorus while Lil Gorilla and two flamingos taught them the Connected Dance. Following his lead, the crowd practiced a couple of times. Señor then said "Drop that beat!"

SONG LYRICS—WE ARE ALL CONNECTED

CHORUS

Woah Woah Woah
Woah Woah Woah
Woah Woah Woah
We Are ALL Connected!

Woah Woah Woah
Woah Woah Woah
Woah Woah Woah
We Are ALL Connected!

VERSE 1

We're on a circular planet
We're peanut butter jamming
From city to the hamlet
All sisters brothers, Janet
Or Myco, like water or land it's
All related in the same sand pit
So don't hate, don't panic
Even though these stages are dramatic
Don't say that we're damaged
One world praying like a mantis
We're faster than the internet
Connected like a magnet
This camera's so candid
A great ship that we captain in'
Work song turn to a ballad hit
Everybody's happiness
Many parties, happy kids
Imagine this nation gripped
Like the way flowers picked
Pictures of us all in the sunset
Across the earth, shine oneness
Life is togetherness

CHORUS

Woah Woah Woah
Woah Woah Woah
Woah Woah Woah
We Are ALL Connected!
Woah Woah Woah
Woah Woah Woah
Woah Woah Woah
We Are ALL Connected!

VERSE 2

We do the connected dance
As we hold our hands
Like a message crammed
In a bottle of sand
A buck, a dough, a wing or a clam
Make shelter, birth babes, take trams
Cross oceans, deserts & lands
Hip-hopopopotomus' we stand
As one, part of me is part of you can't
Never be apart from the same jam
Connected like artists to the fans
A cat's cakewalk or a goat's baa baa'in'
It's the last that comes first again
The blast of the drum, sky to the land
Laugh of the young, sea the ocean
Dancing creator to creation
With the tides, flying like penguins
The fire dreams of ice & cream

The elements combine till everyone sing

CHORUS

Woah Woah Woah
Woah Woah Woah
Woah Woah Woah
We Are ALL Connected!
Woah Woah Woah
Woah Woah Woah
Woah Woah Woah
We Are ALL Connected!

Lyrics by Aaron Ableman

The entire stadium sung "We Are ALL Connected." Afterward Señor spoke about how all beings are connected through Pachamama, the web of life and our shared destiny. He stressed the importance of working together even when everything seems to want to pull us apart. That's why the truce was so important.

Pacha got chills down her spine when he said "Just as we rebuilt this stadium, we can rebuild the world, so long as we do it together." In closing, Señor spoke of a time when all of Nature's children would dance together for the earth!

Pacha said to herself, "Maybe Earth Day."

CHAPTER 15

STOP, ROCK AND ROLL!

hile everyone was prepping for the next performers on stage, Lil Gorilla told Señor, "I don't mean to be a downer, but Mr. Tick is still out there, and he is planning an attack on the Jungle stage to break the truce! The last thing he wants is for us to realize that we're all connected..."

The mushroom turned fire red with anger. When he calmed down, he checked in with his friends in the mycelium network. They suggested Pacha enroll Pebble and his rock friends in the action team for stopping the attack.

In a pile of rocks, they found Pebble cracking jokes. When Pebble heard the news, he suggested that they should be patient, as the President of the United States of AmeRocka would soon be arriving. Speaking at PACHA JAMMA was his special gift to the festival on behalf of the mineral kingdom. "In times like these, it is essential that we remain solid."

Sure enough, within a quarter turn of the sun, Mr. President arrived at the stadium with hundreds of stones following him for autographs. Mr. President even took a picture with Pebble, thanking him for all his hard work and the invitation to PACHA JAMMA. "Imagine that!" thought Pacha! "An ordinary sandstone getting respect from the greatest rock in the history of rocks!"

FUN FACT

Can big things come from small pebbles?

Pebbles may be small, but they're hugely important. Pebble tools are some of the earliest known human-made artifacts dating from the Paleolithic period (hundreds of thousands of years ago). Pebbles show the story of the local geology (rocks) of a place and are actually tiny versions of large mountains.

• •

Mr. President took the stage and as he spoke, a huge roar swept across the stadium. While the crowd chanted and rocked out, Lil Gorilla asked Pebble if he would join the action team to stop the wasps. Pebble wasn't sure what rocks could do to stop the wasps but agreed to try to get some of his rock family to come.

After the President left, three beautiful rocks—Ruby, Emerald, and Citrine—sang "It's All Love," a song about the feeling of love that was in the air at PACHA JAMMA.

SONG LYRICS—IT'S ALL LOVE

CHORUS

It's all love
All life
We're gonna shake down up, up
All right
Stage dive jump, jump
All night

VERSE 1

You're the earthly heaven
You're the juice of fruit
You're the royal crown
To the kingdom in you
You're the map to be found
For the lost in route
When up was down
And right left out

You tuned up the sound
And moved the crowd
Shoutin' all for one
one for all!
Here we go world
the time is now
in the light or dark
all is love, love is all
as the earth turns round
round and round
it's love all around
it's love all around!

BRIDGE

Ruby had a little love
A little love
Little love
Ruby had a little love
Who's face was bright as gold

VERSE 2

Love like birds
As we fly the earth
Surf like pearls
As the tide flow bursts
Stage dive jump
Like we ride the surge
Electric slide down
Shake rumps & swerve
Splash like fountains
One love countin'

Lions on a prowl and
Fields turn fertile
Seed to a flower
Dog to a circle
Happy is the cow for
It's all love's power

CHORUS
It's all love
All life
We're gonna shake down up
All right
Stage dive jump
All night

VERSE 3
Love's a bear with a growl
Holier than mackerel
Gave wings to the owl
Gave roses their smell
Taught the bees all how
To king and queen and crown
Made green from blue and yellow
Took the ant farm to town
Gave pop it's culture
A sweetness and sound
Love is never out of style
Love is never out of style

CHORUS
It's all love
All life

We're gonna shake down up
All right
Stage dive jump
All night

Lyrics by Aaron Ableman

Afterward, Jag roared and Wilder breeched as they took the stage, thanking everyone for a great day. Pacha felt a flurry of conflicting emotions. She was feeling worried and excited, and connected yet sneaky. She paused for a moment, breathing and stretching. The wasp attack would take place soon and Pacha braced herself. She noticed changes in her body. Her breath was shallow, her heartbeat rapid, and her face was sweaty under the mask. She really wanted to take it off but was too afraid to do so.

For the first time, she felt uncomfortable in her PJs. "How do I want to be right now?" she asked herself. But answers did not come. So she asked herself, "What story do I want to tell Mama and Papa about when I get back home?" Then her inner warrior kicked in! She saw that everything, even flubbing her speech, was a lesson preparing her for this very moment. She smiled inside, feeling comfortable in her PJs again. She was eager to do whatever she could to help.

The next day, Pebble, Plat, and Lil Gorilla went to the Jungle Stage to meet the primates. To their distress, only a third of the primates and a handful of rocks showed up. The wise old chimp explained that most of the primates were recovering from a blowout after-party at the Jungle Stage. And apparently the other critters they had invited had forgotten about the meeting entirely. Pacha was surprised and disappointed that the animals weren't taking this more seriously.

Just when Pacha was about to say something, she realized that a Palo Santo tree and three huge Australian tree ferns had joined the group. Then a flurry of stones skipped over to the gathering. Her heart fluttered when Hum zipped up.

Lil Gorilla addressed the group: "Thank you so much for coming. As you know, Mr. Tick is planning a wasp attack on the Jungle Stage during tomorrow's Primate Games."

"Mr. Tick wants to break the truce and keep the web of life divided," said the Palo Santo tree. "But PACHA JAMMA and the primates' efforts to change the dream of humanity are challenging the story he is selling the parasite network. That is why he's coming after the Jungle Stage!"

"Well said!" Lil Gorilla exclaimed. "Who has some ideas?" No one spoke up. "Don't jump in all at once. Seriously, we need a plan."

"Frankly, I'm only here because of Pebble," one of the rocks said. "I don't know anything about insects."

"You saw how slow we move," a tree fern said. "I don't know how we'd help stop those speedy wasps." A couple of rocks even skipped off. Pacha winced and imagined Mr. Tick cackling like he did in the cave. And she could tell that, like her, most of the primates were terrified.

Some of the younger orangutans, however, suggested that the tree ferns donate their largest fronds to make giant fly—er, wasp—swatters, but no one thought that would work.

It was then that Plat spoke up. "Each and every one of you has a different gift! Trees are tall, rocks are hard, hummingbirds are fast flyers, Palo Santo is aromatic, mushrooms are great communicators, primates are smart (when they aren't being dumb), and platypuses, I mean platypi, are pretty adaptable."

"Actually, I think it is 'platypuses,'" Lil Gorilla said.

Plat grinned. "I think us platypi know what we're called."

That drew some smiles. "I don't have a clue what exactly we should do," Plat said, "but I do know this" and he started to sing.

SONG LYRICS—USE WHAT YOU GOT

VERSE 1

I spent my life searching for my beauty
Left behind, Lord, in my own movie
But my love, I found in the bottom of the sea
I didn't know what I had until I believed
I've always heard that ocean's too big (too big)
Too many fishes, tides too rough and dying to live
But my heart beat's like the music
So if you don't know, then you've got to know, you've got to use it

CHORUS

You've got to use, got to use
Use what you got
You've got to use, use what you got
You've got to use, use what you got

VERSE 2

I always dreamed of love
Called and screamed for love
My job was freedom cuz
The river seemed to tug
Me down when I was up
Too fast or slow my luck
Called me chicken cluck
But now, now's my time to shine above

And if you call me platypus
I'll never never never duck
I'll never never never duck
We're all shining (all shining)
I do the duck dance

CHORUS

You've got to use, got to use
Use what you got
You've got to use, use what you got
You've got to use, use what you got

Lyrics by Aaron Ableman

The other animals clapped, singing the choruses with Plat and doing the Duck Dance. "These crazy critters never miss a chance to party," Pacha thought to herself.

When the song was done, Plat took a bow. "You each have everything you need within yourself. You are whole, perfect, and complete. And together we have everything we need to create the world we want to live in. We just need to figure out how our gifts can work together to serve the highest good—protecting the truce, PACHA JAMMA, and Pachamama!"

Pacha was glowing inside. "Thanks Plat! I think I have an idea and it involves all of us. But I need some time to map it all out. Unless you hear differently, everyone meet me here at the Jungle Stage tomorrow afternoon. And primates, please bring as many of your friends as possible. Same goes to the rocks and trees. Hum, please ask the bees and wasps to come. Señor, please bring me two bags of red clay tomorrow."

As the plants and animals made their way back to their campsites, Lil Gorilla stayed to survey the stage. The Jungle Stage was actually a theater in the round, featuring a circular stage surrounded by many circles of seats, none farther than 50 feet from the stage. The stage could rotate in either direction and change speeds. The theater was surrounded by large redwood and sequoia trees with hemp rope platforms that served as balcony seating for the alpha males and their mates. Pacha did a full sketch of the stage on a piece of papyrus.

CHAPTER 16

USE WHAT YOU GOT

That night was a restless one for Pacha. She stayed up late planning and plotting the defense of the Jungle Stage. And even when she wanted to go to sleep, the ideas kept on coming. When she finally calmed her mind, she had a vision of her *abuelita* offering encouragement and kind words. She knew she was on the right track.

When Pacha arrived at the Jungle Stage that afternoon with Hum, she was pleasantly surprised that the entire team showed up with their families. They were 108 primates, more than 300 rocks, 12 tree ferns, six Palo Santos, and thousands of bees and wasps. Pacha was overjoyed to see Señor and his mushroom posse slide up with a bucket of red clay in tow.

"Thank you all for coming! I think we've got everything we need." She asked them to smear the red clay paste on each other. "My papa told me to wear red in the garden at school because bees and wasps cannot see red."

Next she asked the Palo Santo trees to sacrifice their smallest branches and twigs. With the same care they use when they groom their own, the primates trimmed the Palo Santo trees and stacked several hundred small bundles of the wood. The tree ferns waved their fronds to cool down the clay-covered primates as they worked.

Lil Gorilla then had the orangutans sort out flat and bowl-shaped rocks while the chimps, bonobos, apes, and four tiny lemurs gathered clumps of moss from the forest. They were careful to always ask the moss for permission and only take a humble amount. Lil Gorilla, with Hum and Señor's assistance, then positioned the larger primates around the outside of the Jungle Stage. Each one was armed with two smooth stones, a bowl-shaped rock with a clump of moss, and a bundle of Palo Santo twigs. She arranged the lemurs in a smaller circle closer to the stage and told the larger primates to watch the lemurs for the signal. Next she positioned the 12 tree ferns around the stage. She

had her bee and wasp friends wait in nearby trees. Lil Gorilla, Hum, Plat and Señor each took a position at the edge of the stage so that one of them could alert the lemurs no matter which direction the jewel wasps attacked from.

About an hour later, Pacha heard a low hum. At first she thought it might be the crowd, but she remembered that peculiar sound from the tunnels beneath the mountains. Strangely the buzzing did not get louder. Pacha locked eyes with Hum for a moment and Hum flew off to investigate. She was gone for just a minute before she frantically zipped to Pacha's side.

"A huge cloud of wasps is circling the stage like giant donut!"

Pacha was surprised and alarmed. Had there been a change in Mr. Tick's plans? She asked Hum what direction the wasps were circling and Hum said clockwise. "The stage is moving clockwise as well," she said to herself. "I bet the wasps are confused by the rotation of the stage."

Mama had always taught Pacha to experiment and change plans if it's not working. To test her theory, Lil Gorilla asked the chimpanzee stagehands to change the direction of the stage to go the other way while Hum flew off to observe the wasp cloud. Sure enough, the wasps also changed the direction of their circling. "This is going to work even better than I thought!" Pacha exclaimed. She asked the chimps to keep the stage rotating for the moment.

"I've grown up with the smell of Palo Santo at home," Pacha whispered to the jittery Hum. "But I didn't understand its power until my *abuelita* taught me about smudging. She showed me how to clear a space of what she called 'hucha,' or heavy energy, with the smoke."

Lil Gorilla and Hum made their way over to the Palo Santo trees, who were still wincing from giving away so many of their branches and twigs. Pacha thanked the Palo Santo trees again for their help. "May we clear the Jungle Stage and all PACHA JAMMA of this deadly wasp *hucha,* and

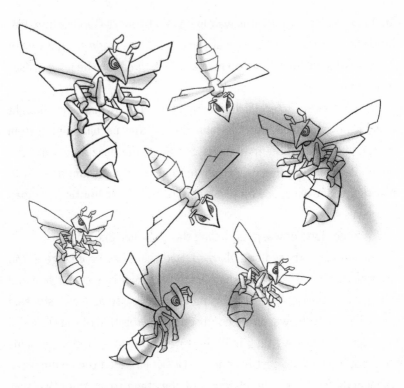

the fear and separation it brings, so that we may create a field of peace, connectedness and love! *Axé. Aho! Amen!*"

With tears welling in her eyes, Lil Gorilla signaled to the lemurs. The lemurs signaled to the larger primates, who clacked their rocks together. The rocks created sparks that dropped onto the moss in the rock bowls and smoldered. The primates blew on their smoldering moss clump until they caught fire and then lit their bundles of Palo Santo.

As the Palo Santo smoke rose, the giant tree ferns waved their fronds, fanning the smoke into a dome hovering between the stage and the wasps.

Lil Gorilla then had the chimpanzees stop the stage.

Pacha watched as the donut of wasps attacked from all directions. But as soon as the wasps hit the Palo Santo smoke, they fluttered

aimlessly about, falling in love with each other on the spot. Meanwhile, Hum signaled to her pollinator friends to take the love struck jewel wasps safely away and welcome them back into the pollinator community. Afterward, the entire team gathered to give thanks and celebrate their triumph!

CHAPTER 17

THE FINAL DANCE

The next day whizzed by for Lil Gorilla as she bounced around the festival, in and out of the stadium. She was a little nervous about her performance, but much less than she might have expected. Being the last performer of the festival, she was excused from her other duties for the day and actually had a chance to spend some time in the stands. She was inspired by talking to the spectators seeing the festival from their perspective.

She was especially excited by a conversation she overheard between the two flamingo sisters who had sung the chorus of "We Are All Connected" on stage. The sisters were reflecting on how the storm actually brought everyone together. When one of the sisters said the only thing missing at PACHA JAMMA was the "hairless apes," Pacha's heart skipped a beat. She got goose bumps when the pink flamingo exclaimed, "Making the world a better place is going to take ALL OF US, including the hairless apes." The orange flamingo sighed. "I guess that'll have to wait until next year."

Maybe not, Pacha thought.

Later that evening, a white buffalo, a snow lion, and a llama appeared on stage as if emerging from thin air! They wowed the Faux News photographers, who took thousands of pictures. After the photos stopped flashing and the applause started to wane, the llama spoke:

"Thank you for welcoming me. I bring greetings and congratulations from the newly constituted Council of All Beings. The new council formed organically here from the work of the Connectedness Action Team, which held listening sessions at all the different Action Stages. We found that PACHA JAMMA is part of an awakening that has been emerging for decades. Billions of us share many values that orient our lives in a common direction—regardless of our species or the habitat we live in.

"While our practices and beliefs are many, we share knowledge about the greatest challenges to the earth and a resolve to work together to ensure a healthy planet for the entire web of life. Between now and the next PACHA JAMMA, we hope to go forward from a truce to a real treaty so we can all help shift the dream of humanity and heal Pachamama in full.

"And now it's time for the final performance. A grand finale with the now famous Lil Gorilla!"

Pacha was feeling the fate of the planet in her body. Her nerves jangled like she was walking on thin ice. But something pushed her forward, calling her to face her fears of speaking before this huge crowd. Plus, the festival had survived a super storm and a brain-controlling wasp attack—if she didn't perform she'd be called a scaredy-cat by the lions and tigers!

But just as the DJ Octopus queued up the track for her performance, Pacha realized that something had snuck onto her shoulder! Ack! It was none other than Mr. Tick himself!

"I'm taking your slot, Lil Ms. Wheezer! I knew you were a human from the first taste...and if you don't let me take the spotlight, I'll spill the beans! This whole festival has been a disaster for me and it's all your fault! Consider yourself lucky that I don't take a bite out of you right now."

In the past, Pacha might have frozen in fear or lost her breath, but now closed her eyes to find her center! Pacha remembered to count backwards from five to one. She tuned into her breathing and straightened her spine. She realized that she was tapping into an inner strength and courage that she didn't usually notice but was always there.

Pacha chose to let go of her fears. She realized that she had the power to stop this little luna-tick from stealing the joy out of life. As Mr. Tick continued babbling threats, Pacha calmly walked over to the security

area and, with the flick of her finger, knocked Mr. Tick off of her shoulder into a Venus flytrap. The flower closed its jaws, locking Mr. Tick up in his own personal "box seat". Luckily for Mr. Tick, the carnivorous flower was observing the truce like everyone else at Pacha Jamma. Lil Gorilla asked the flower to let Mr. Tick go once the show was over, to give him a chance to change...like everyone else in the world.

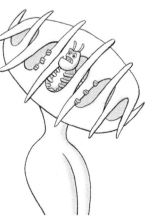

As Mr. Tick screamed in frustration, the stadium microphone announced:

"One more time, please give it up for Lil Gorilla!"

Lil Gorilla did her best superstar walk out onto the stage, waving and blowing kisses while the crystal strobe lights flashed. She felt more confident than ever, having stopped that wicked tick once and for all. Somehow her stage fright was nowhere to be found. She was in her element!

Lil Gorilla went on to do an "evolution of dance":

...she did the worm...
she did the funky chicken
she did the hound-dog...
she did amazing backflips across the stage!
She did the Roger Rabbit
the Humpty Hump...
...she did a wild version of the Monkey!
She Whipped and Nae Naed...
She even moonwalked in the moonlight!

The crowd went crazy with laughter and amazement!

It was like watching Myco Jackson
for the first time—jaw dropping!

The peanut gallery
was going nuts.

CHAPTER 18

WHO I REALLY AM

At the end of her dance performance, however, Pacha felt everything go into slow motion, though the audience didn't have a clue. She saw how much everyone loved her dancing and it confirmed for her, something that she had felt all along, that maybe she didn't need to hide behind the gorilla mask after all.

"Either they love me as I am or...well...I don't want cheers for something I'm not!" Pacha thought as she did a final moonwalk and toe stand.

As Lil Gorilla lowered to her feet, she threw off her mask in a gesture of triumph. The crowd went totally silent in shock. Lil Gorilla wasn't a gorilla after all—she was a little Girl-rilla! The audience began whispering in many languages: "...it's a human... it's a human... it's a human..."

The whispers slowly turned to murmurs of appreciation all around her—Hum and the flamingos flapping their wings, Jag clapping his paws, Tree's branches creaking, Wilder the Whale breeching, Pebble cracking up, and Señor whooping. More and more plants and animals joined in, and soon the entire crowd was roaring. Pacha was almost as amazed as the audience. Then from somewhere deep inside, she found the courage to speak her truth.

"I am a child of Nature...like all of you. Your dream is my dream too." There was silence across the stadium.

"It's been a long journey to get here and I've faced many obstacles, but I'm not afraid any more! I'm not afraid of who I am! I am Pacha!"

You could hear a feather fall or a dragonfly flap its wings. Many in the audience began to sniffle. Jag stepped forward and gently put his paw on Pacha's shoulder. "Child," he whispered in her ear, "you are so much more than you know. In my tradition, the word pacha signifies the One Life force that flows through everything. Pacha means oneness!"

At that very moment, Pacha realized what Señor had been trying to tell her earlier with his hot dog joke. She was to ask the teacher to "make her one with everything," and indeed he had. With teary eyes, she put her arm around the sneaky mushroom, who laughed and hugged her back.

The brawny feline then surveyed the audience and roared, "I have a dream that one day all of Nature will be honored as equal! There is no doubt in my mind that our beloved mother Pachamama loves all of you for who you are! It's a dream come true to bring together all species... Pacha being human makes this festival complete!"

He smiled at Pacha before turning back to the crowd. "Now let's get the rest of the human family to honor Mother Earth and stop troubling this precious home of ours. Will you dream with me? Will you dream for freedom? Let freedom sing!"

FUN FACT

Does Nature have rights?

Nature's Rights means that species and ecosystems have legal rights to exist, flourish, and naturally evolve.

Here are a few new (and old) laws that come from Ecuador and Bolivia:

- Mother Earth is a living being.
- Mother Earth is a unique community of beings that sustains all beings.
- Each being is important because of its relationships.
- The rights of Mother Earth are basic, like human rights, and are deserved because humans and nature share the same source of existence.

• •

Pacha realized that Pachamama had called her here to be humanity's messenger. She saw how going around the world to gather the primates and all of her experiences at PACHA JAMMA were just part of her inner journey to know herself and her gifts. For the first time she could remember, Pacha finally felt comfortable in her skin.

"I've learned from all of you that together we can make a better world, and that begins with knowing ourselves!" Pacha cried. "And we have to use what we got! I see now that change starts from within and ripples out in beautiful ways, aiding others in ways that we may never know. We are all sharing one planet and humans like me need to start acting like it!"

"How can humans do that, Ms. Girl-illa?" asked Hum, hovering over her shoulder.

"Sometimes I think we forget that there *are* many humans who are making change! I have asthma but I am learning to breathe easier; to pause and let my awareness catch up with my monkey mind. If I can change, so can humanity." She closed her eyes and paused for a moment. These words came to her: "Let's all take a deep breath together!"

Pacha led the whole stadium to breathe together at once. With her eyes still closed, her voice cracked a little. "When we breathe together we realize we are single beings on this journey, and at the same time, connected to one another, animated by the same life energy that is in the petal of an orchid, the howl of the wolf, the spirit of Pachamama.

"It's only a few human ideas that are the root of our problems. Now is the time for Pachamama's spirit to sing clearly through humanity. So we can learn to love ourselves, to stop fighting, and remember we're actually one earth family! Every day we can bring our favorite songs to the concert of life!"

The audience chirped, purred, and howled in agreement. Pacha couldn't have been happier!

"I can't wait for the next PACHA JAMMA," Hum chirped, "so we can grow this seed into a mighty tree with fruit for all. When you all finally make it back home, remember that you are part of a huge burst of positive change that will ripple all around the world."

With that, an eagle and a condor flew together over the stage and into the starry night. Nature sang a song so dazzling that all the children of humanity heard the call in their dreams. All the dreamers were invited to join the party and change the world, and so they did...starting with themselves.

Finally, like all the other children, Pacha woke up in her own bedroom with a giggle. She took a deep breath and felt like the whole world was dancing within her. She danced across her bedroom to the mirror and laughed when she saw that the mushroom on her PJs was winking at her! Pacha was ready to bring her big dreams to life.

SONG LYRICS—PACHA'S THEME

CHORUS

Pacha's Pajamas comes to life

It's a story

Where we all unite

It's a dream upon

A starry night

Take a deep breath

Cuz the air is fresh

Bring your instruments

To the nature fest

VERSE 1

Come on everybody

Let's have a party

Let's get down

With the freshest sound

Come check the story

Chart the journey

Dance it now

Where the music is found

Oooh she gotcha

Her name is Pacha

And this is whale

With the hugest tale

Good great beats

It's a tree's belief
The bestest dreams come true

CHORUS

Pacha's Pajamas comes to life
It's a story
Where we all unite
It's a dream upon
A starry night
Take a deep breath
Cuz the air is fresh
Bring your instruments
To the nature fest

VERSE 2

The bestest dreams come true
Pebble will you rock you
Duck bill with splash too
It's a roar of a Jaguar
The poise of Spider
Nature can talk, word?
It's a butterfly world
So fly like a Hummingbird
Shine with the Jacksuns
Time with the rap, ah
Come on rover, come on clover
It's a real sleepover

CHORUS

Pacha's Pajamas comes to life
It's a story
Where we all unite

It's a dream upon
A starry night
Take a deep breath
Cuz the air is fresh
Bring your instruments
To the nature fest

Lyrics by Aaron Ableman

EPILOGUE

For months after her dream adventure, Pacha had gotten along much better with that crazy Ms. Wheezer, mainly because Ms. Wheezer wasn't coming around as often. Even when Ms. Wheezer seemed especially determined to visit, Pacha usually figured out ways to avoid her by pausing and pacing herself like she did at PACHA JAMMA.

Pacha was counting her blessings—one of her new habits—as she collected trash in the park to turn into art and science

FUN FACT

Got Vitamin N?

It's the vitamin for Nature. Without it, you run the risk of getting Nature Deficit Disorder. That's what it's called when kids don't have access to nature or spend too much time staring at screens. Some of the effects are a short attention span or being depressed a lot. This is an important reminder to all of us that we need to be close to nature. It's like eating or drinking, but for your spirit. Besides, an ocean or a forest is still the best playground, and a sunset can be better than any TV show!

• •

experiments. She had almost filled her entire bag when she caught a hint of Ms. Wheezer. Unsure of whether it was the truck exhaust or her nervousness about the performance she was to do the next day, Pacha decided to take a breather under the tree where she liked to practice clearing her mind and stretching.

This particular day, pajamas were on her mind. For one, the characters on her pajamas were sleeping later and later. They looked so peaceful sleeping but she was starting to miss them. And the other day, Pacha caught a glimpse in the mirror of an empty space on the back of her pajama leg where Wilder the Whale had been swimming lately. But as these thoughts came to her mind, she just let them pass and refocused on her breath.

Just as she was breathing evenly, several kids passed by, laughing and joking. One of them dropped a plastic hamburger container on the ground in front of Pacha without breaking stride.

Before she knew what she was doing, Pacha hopped up, and shouted "Hey!" The kids turned and stopped.

A boy with a turned-back baseball cap squinted in Pacha's direction. "Yeah, what's up?" he asked. Pacha saw it was Aaron from school. She wasn't sure what exactly she wanted to say but she knew she had to say something.

She picked up the plastic container. "I think one of you may have dropped this. I'm really careful about plastic these days," she continued, her voice growing in confidence. "'Cause you never know where it could end up, like a bird's stomach or a whale's blowhole."

"Who cares what you think?" said the boy who dropped the container. "Who do you think you are, anyway?"

"I'm Pacha," she said proudly. "It means 'earth,' which I'm here to protect. And you should be too."

Aaron's eyes lit up. "Whoa! I had this awesome dream a few months ago. There was a huge dance party in nature with plants, animals, and kids from everywhere. I was rapping with a platypus, a beatboxing chicken, and a hippopotamus...We were talking about being connected as one earth family!"

Pacha grinned and gave him a high ten. "Your dream is my dream too!"

Turning to his friend, Pacha handed the plastic container to its slightly red-faced owner. "I guess you could throw it away...but where is 'away' anyway? It would bev much better to turn it into art like I do or recycle it at least. Not too mention that hamburgers and factory-farms are causing climate chaos!"

She shifted her focus to the entire group. "I did a social experiment last month called the Plastic Challenge, where my family tried to reduce our plastic waste. It was pretty tough to do, especially for my parents, but these days we're using much less, recycling more, and reusing whenever we can. You could too."

As Pacha started to walk away, she was smiling inside. She felt like she was making beautiful music in the concert of life. Her dreams were encouraging her to do things she hadn't even thought of.

Without thinking, she turned back to the kids. "By the way, I had a vision of a global dance party that brings us all together! How about we do a flash mob...in our pajamas?"

CONNECTED DANCE

CHALLENGE

Submit a video of you and your friends
doing the Connected Dance with Pacha

Scan here to find out about
current prizes and the chance to be
in videos with kids around the world!

Pacha's Priorities

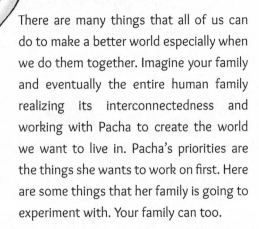

- ✓ Youth Leadership
- ✓ Reforestation
- ✓ Healthy Soil
- ✓ Litter Free

There are many things that all of us can do to make a better world especially when we do them together. Imagine your family and eventually the entire human family realizing its interconnectedness and working with Pacha to create the world we want to live in. Pacha's priorities are the things she wants to work on first. Here are some things that her family is going to experiment with. Your family can too.

1. REDUCE
   - Make less waste
   - Reduce plastic consumption (e.g., products with a lot of packaging)
   - Cut down on factory-farmed meat consumption
2. CONSERVE
   - Turn off lights

- Turn down heater/AC
- Turn off and unplug electronic devices
- Keep doors and windows closed
- Use blinds and drapes
- Engage in activities that involve less energy or transportation
- Run the dishwasher and washing machine only when there's a full load
- Wash clothes with cold water
- Hang clothes to dry instead of running the dryer

3. PLANT
   - Plant a tree perhaps using one of Pacha's Tree Kits
   - Plant a veggie garden or a fruit tree at your home
   - Join a community garden
   - Ask your school to plant a garden that produces veggies for school lunch

Below are some organizations that Pacha and her family think are awesome!

Get inspired and empowered by stories of young hero/ines of today and join their actions!

YOUTH-LEADER unites more than 100 teenage changemakers from around the planet on one platform, to equip young people, teachers and parents with their solutions, tools, tricks, and even "live" meetings - to learn and take action on issues they are most passionate about.

Inspired students can form student clubs and join a global community of like-hearted youth. They can even make changemaking their full-time sport and lifestyle with a groundbreaking reality game—CHANGE GENERATION RISING—taking monthly missions aligned with International Days of the United Nations—like youth, oceans, forests, water, street children, also Shark Week, and of course—the International Day of Talking Like a Pirate!

Actions range from fundraisers and book drives to fun lifestyle challenges and massive projects, designed to shape history. Don't forget—this is done in partnership with the greatest changemakers of our time, the pacemakers of the Change Generation, and you are invited to write this exciting new chapter in human history with them.

Find out more at www.youth-leader.org and www.cgrising.com

KISS
~ the ~
GROUND

Hey kids! Did you know that healthy food comes from healthy soil? Healthy soil also helps save water, keep our habitats alive, and can pull huge amounts of excess CO2 out of the atmosphere to bring our climate back into balance.

Want to help? You, me, your mom and dad, and everyone you know can help nature build back Healthy Soil by composting food scraps. We provide information for you to share with your community about the importance of taking care of our soil. Our videos and infographics make it simple so kids like you can learn about the benefits of soil and do your part to help build it back.

Thanks for Kissing The Ground with us.

www.kisstheground.com

Imagine ForestNation...Imagine a world where everyone grows their own trees.

Just imagine if schools and their students encourage their local communities to grow their own trees. Now imagine that another tree gets planted in a developing country to match each of these trees. This would have a massive social and environmental impact around the world. You can become a citizen of ForestNation by growing your own tree and we'll plant another one in a developing country.

It will help us connect with nature, and help us all connect with each other.

www.forestnation.com

It's everywhere. Laying in our streets. Stranded on our beaches. Floating in our oceans. Litter is so widespread that it blends into the background of our lives. And with seven billion of us sharing the planet, the problem is only getting worse. Changing the world means changing our behavior and there's no better time to start than childhood. Schools are using Litterati as a citizen-science tool to gain a better understanding of our impact on the planet, and more importantly, think about solutions for creating a litter-free world.

www.litterati.org

We are a tribe of young activists, artists and musicians from across the globe stepping up as leaders and co-creating the future we know is possible. We are the ones we've been waiting for.

We are #GenerationRyse!

We are growing movement with youth at the forefront by empowering them as leaders and amplifying their impact. Join us!

www.earthguardians.org

CLIMATE PARENTS

Hey Parents!

Kids like Pacha need grownups like you to take action to implement solutions to climate change! Pacha's generation is counting on our initiative and leadership.

Climate change is harming kids and communities, fueling the droughts, wildfires and super storms afflicting much of our country. And carbon pollution contributes to soaring rates of childhood asthma.

Climate Parents is mobilizing parents and families to push policy makers and energy companies to stop prioritizing dirty energy, and to scale up "kid-safe and climate-safe" energy instead. For us to succeed, we need parents like you to get involved. Join us!

www.climateparents.org

 ## Pachamama Alliance

Hi Parents! Pacha is inspired by the Pachamama Alliance, and its work to change the dream of humanity. Pachamama Alliance is a global community that offers people the chance to learn, connect, engage, travel and cherish life for the purpose of creating a sustainable future that works for all.

Our intention is to generate a critical mass of conscious commitment. With roots deep in the Amazon rainforest, our programs integrate indigenous wisdom with modern knowledge to support personal, and collective, transformation that is the catalyst to bringing forth an environmentally sustainable, spiritually fulfilling, socially just human presence on this planet.

http://pachamama.org/engage

This is how we'll plant Billions of Trees!

Tree Kits - You Plant We Plant

Everything you need to grow your own trees at home.
Plastic-free biodegradable packaging and ForestNation
plants matching trees in developing countries!

The Greenest School Fundraiser

Sell Tree Kits. It is really easy to start!
Fundraise anyway you like with any profit
margin you need.

For more information, visit treekit.pachaspajamas.com

DREAM JOURNAL

Our dreams are a window into our subconscious mind. Dreams can help us understand ourselves, find our purpose, and choose the best course of action. Sometimes they show us a possible future; many dreaming traditions believe you also can do things in waking life or the dreamtime to create the possible future you prefer. Dream Incubation and Dream Reflection are methods for getting the most out of dreamtime. Both methods are based on the book THE THREE "ONLY" THINGS: Tapping the Power of Dreams, Coincidence, and Imagination by Robert Moss (www.mossdreams.com).

Enjoy recording and sharing dreams among friends and family, and explore what they would do if it were their dream. Playacting your dreams with others can also be powerful. It's a great activity for parents to do with younger kids. For more info, visit http://pachaspajamas.com/dream-journaling.

May your best dreams come true!

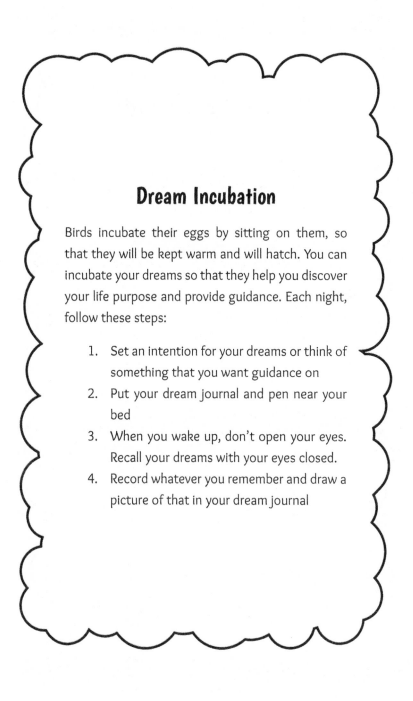

Dream Incubation

Birds incubate their eggs by sitting on them, so that they will be kept warm and will hatch. You can incubate your dreams so that they help you discover your life purpose and provide guidance. Each night, follow these steps:

1. Set an intention for your dreams or think of something that you want guidance on
2. Put your dream journal and pen near your bed
3. When you wake up, don't open your eyes. Recall your dreams with your eyes closed.
4. Record whatever you remember and draw a picture of that in your dream journal

Dream Reflection/Sharing

A Message from Pacha:

Hey Dream Scouts! I'm trying out a new dream reflection and sharing practice and I invite you to try it with me. Will you pledge to do as much of this as you can with whatever you recall from your dreamtime for a week or more. Remember to be kind to snippets. Sometimes the one thing that you remember is what you need the most at that moment,

Here's what Pacha is doing:

1. Pacha names her Dream, and jots down the date and whether it was a night dream, day dream, or somewhere in between. She also notes what crystal she put under her pillow. Pacha has always liked rocks. She is trying out a rose quartz now.
2. She notes the story of the dream - just the facts.

3. She reflects on three questions
   - How am I feeling about the dream?
   - Reality Check: What do I recognize from this dream from real life, and what parts of this dream could be played out in the future?
   - What more do I want to know about this dream?
4. Pacha loves feedback from other Dream Scouts. You can get feedback from friends and family about what they would do if this were their dream
5. Pacha chooses an action. She asks herself What am I going to do now? Her abuelita taught her that she must do something to honor the dreams so they keep coming back. It can be something as small as you want it to be. The other day, Pacha ate a red apple in waking life because she was riding a firetruck in her dream.
6. Pacha makes a slogan or personal motto to help her integrate the dream into her life.

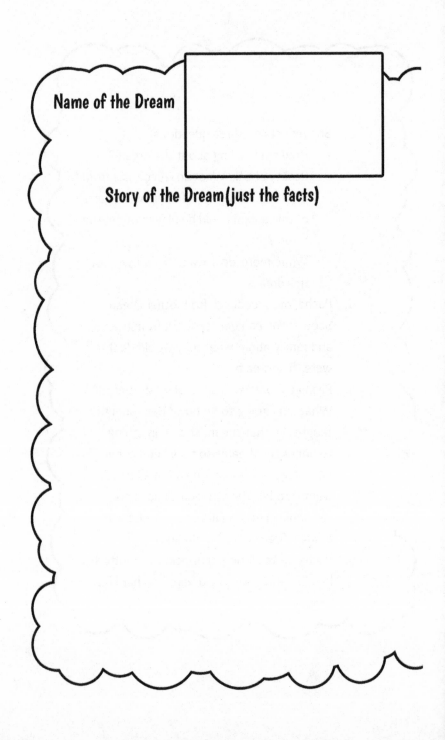

Name of the Dream

Story of the Dream (just the facts)

How are you feeling about the dream?

Reality Check: What do you recognize in this dream from real life, and what parts of this dream could be played out in the future?

What more do you want to know about this dream?

Feedback from friends and family about what they would do if this were their dream

Action: What will you do to honor this dream?

Slogan that captures the message of the dream and orients you towards forward movement

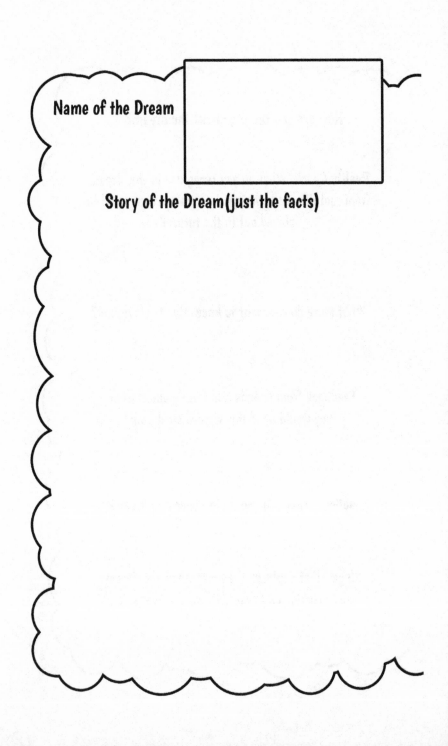

Name of the Dream

Story of the Dream (just the facts)

How are you feeling about the dream?

Reality Check: What do you recognize in this dream from real life, and what parts of this dream could be played out in the future?

What more do you want to know about this dream?

Feedback from friends and family about what they would do if this were their dream

Action: What will you do to honor this dream?

Slogan that captures the message of the dream and orients you towards forward movement

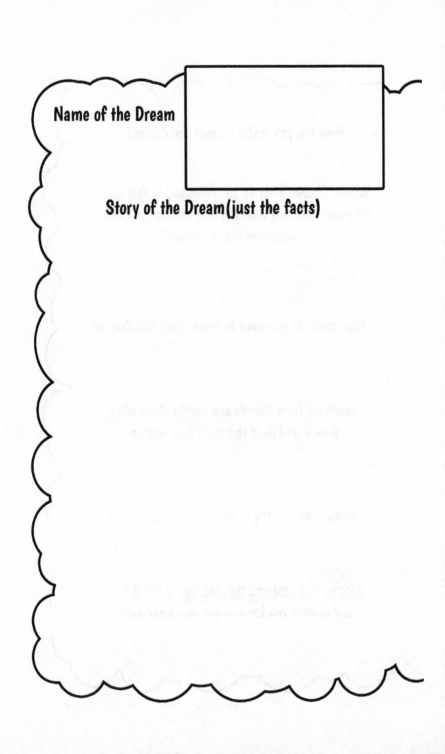

Name of the Dream

Story of the Dream (just the facts)

How are you feeling about the dream?

Reality Check: What do you recognize in this dream from real life, and what parts of this dream could be played out in the future?

What more do you want to know about this dream?

Feedback from friends and family about what they would do if this were their dream

Action: What will you do to honor this dream?

Slogan that captures the message of the dream and orients you towards forward movement

Name of the Dream

Story of the Dream (just the facts)

How are you feeling about the dream?

Reality Check: What do you recognize in this dream from real life, and what parts of this dream could be played out in the future?

What more do you want to know about this dream?

Feedback from friends and family about what they would do if this were their dream

Action: What will you do to honor this dream?

Slogan that captures the message of the dream and orients you towards forward movement

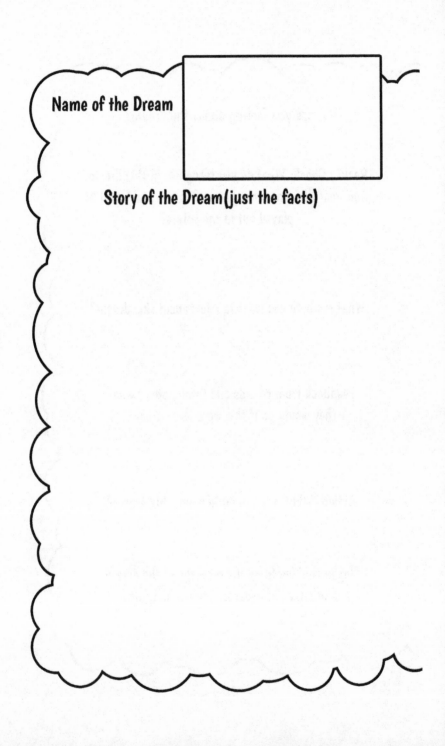

Name of the Dream

Story of the Dream (just the facts)

How are you feeling about the dream?

Reality Check: What do you recognize in this dream from real life, and what parts of this dream could be played out in the future?

What more do you want to know about this dream?

Feedback from friends and family about what they would do if this were their dream

Action: What will you do to honor this dream?

Slogan that captures the message of the dream and orients you towards forward movement

We are grateful for our sponsors

ACKNOWLEDGEMENTS

Giving thanks to the Great Spirit of life, that which is beyond name or number. Deep gratitude to the indigenous spirit inside all of us, singing in ancestral voices that remind us to love ourselves, our relatives and the planet upon which we depend. Big love and best wishes to the Ableman family, the Williams family, the Room family, the Jonson family, the Marin family and all of the family energy that has stood behind this project since Day One! Respect for our global community of dreamers—those who have supported this dream in action, from the patient collaborators to the studio engineer's focus to the fire circle of storytellers and musicians calling forth a masterpiece from the heart. Appreciations to Armin Wolf and Christine Schoefer for believing in this vision. Big LOVE to Erika Minkowsky for her angelic support through and through! Big thanks to all of our investors and Kickstarter supporters for rising with us as a collective. Much love to all the kids involved in this project. Appreciations to Rev. Elouise Oliver and the Science Of Mind global community. Gratitude to Clifford Chapman, Samuel Moses, Les Washington, Ken Petersen, Jeff Wallace, Reena Jadhav, Michele Sconiers, Duane Melius, Naru Kwina, Jora Trang, and Najorae, Andreas Smith, Lester Chambers, Rick Ingrasci, Gretchen Krampf, Valdilene Bruno, Dennise Hilliman, John Smith & family, David Hopkins, Andrew Orgel, Suzanne Toro, Lorna Apper, Geoff Smith, Ritu Agarwal, Sue Blythe, Diana Chu, Gretchen Thomas, Maureen Shea, Andrew McGovern of Zahada, Glenna Forster-Jones, Charles Turner, Mariana Johnson Andres, Joe Mohr, Dove Mosis, Dulce Juarez, Kay Cuajanco, Shamini Dhana, Richard Naylor, Colin Miller, Melia Room, Amelía Aeon Karris, Avalon Theisen and family, Q'orianka Kilcher, Gerardo Marin, Irene Bonilla, Ernesto Olmos, Ambessa Cantave, Leif Wold, Acorn Sunbeam, Lynne Elizabeth, Drew Dellinger, Brian Stross, Stephanie Lipow, Alex Hill, Kevin Connelly, Lois Bridges, Winnie Poon, Magalie Bonneau-Marcil, James Nixon, Walter Jackson, David Christopher, Kent Lewandowski, Umi Says, Mark Stafford, Elana Yonah, Rose Yee, Aaron Lehmer, Ryland and Sarah Engleheart, Toiya Finley, @ak2webd3, Linda Parker Pennington, Robin Room, Kevin Jones, Yu-kai Chou, Elisabeth Garst, Raj Ramaya, Susan Silber, Monifa Bandale, Zero Nylin, Dre Jonson, Lev Laltoo and Family, i.am.mani, Shani Wade, Yonatan Landau, Jeff Shiu, Hub Bay Area, Pancho Ramos Stierle, Nipun Mehta, Ricardo Gressel, Ralph Guggenheim, Karen Robert, Jin An Wong, Kat Thompson, Ama Zenya, Sita Davis, Ayse Gursoz, Annie Leonard, Marc Finser, Diana Cohn, Cory Richardson, Pablo Bonjour, Craig Allen, Rahul Iyer, Dayna Reggero, Bud Smith, Victor Douglas, Rich Saleh and everyone between. Big thanks for all the organizational support, networks and inspiration from the Batchery, IGS Mobile, the Fountain, Impact Hub Oakland, Earth Guardians, THinc Green, O'Melveny & Myers, the Global Alliance for Nature's Rights, Green For All, Destiny Arts Center, Ella Baker Center, KPFA, Ankh Marketing, Cafe Gratitude, Global Exchange, Youth Leader, Litterati, Forest Nation, The Master Shift, and Kiss The Ground!

ABOUT THE AUTHORS

Dave Room

My most important identifier is Melia's Papa. My fourteen-year-old daughter Melia is my motivation and inspiration. Before she arrived, I was concerned about how I would relate to an infant. Up until then, I had enjoyed kids that were already talking, but babies always seemed to want to squirm back to their mothers.

When Melia was two weeks old, her mother laid her on my chest. I reveled in the most divine baby smell, feeling grateful to finally be able to relax with my newborn daughter. Over the course of minutes, Melia inched her way up my chest and nuzzled her head into my neck. It felt like I was being cuddled by the cutest, most loving puppy ever.

And then something magical happened. An electric pulse went through my entire body activating every cell of my being. I knew at that moment, this was the most important relationship in my life. Soon thereafter, it came to me—when Melia is a young adult, I need to be able to look her in the eyes and tell her I did everything could to make the world a better place.

This launched me on a decade-long quest to figure out how I would make the world a better place, which ultimately led to starting BALANCE Edutainment with Aaron. Our vision is to create global platforms for engaging children in the planetary awakening that is already underway. Our first global platform is Pacha's Pajamas.

I am passionate about uplifting the voices of children, women, impoverished peoples, indigenous peoples, and Nature to ensure that they play a key role in shaping a future that works for all. I think it is essential that we all look deep within to find our purpose and voice, and to develop our internal guidance system. I see the intersection of entertainment and education as an essential tool for reaching young people where they are at, and supporting their awakening to self-awareness and self-mastery so that they may create the world they want to live in.

Twitter and Instagram: @meliaspapa
Website: http://meliaspapa.com

Aaron Ableman

A celebrated entertainer, author, and entrepreneur, Mr. Ableman grew up under the guidance of a farmer and public-health nurse for parents, studying with luminaries from many walks of life. Born in actor Michael Douglas' basement, Aaron was raised under auspicious conditions.

From his time in Nicaragua at the end of the civil war to being raised on a landmark urban farm, Ableman has held unusual leadership roles since a young age. He was a frequent star in annual stage shows as a child actor and playwright. Since high-school, he has been recognized as a distinguished producer, actor and writer in the fields of music, literature, film and education. Ableman soon began to write and compose musicals under the tutelage of Stanford theatre buff, Ian Cummings, with Nina Simone's producer, Charles Ellison, (Concordia University) and at the renowned Esalen Institute with actress/master teacher, Paula Shaw. At the time, he was asked to be creative director and producer with an arts-education organization called Music Mind Movement. The group grew to national prominence and was a catalyst for many well-known artists across North America.

After university, he travelled as an artist-ambassador and educator reaching 10,000 orphans and low-income school children in the villages of Mumbai and Varanasi, India. Returning to North America to consult with arts-education organizations in Canada, he went on to produce and teach a number of programs for marginalized school-kids. Moving back to California, Ableman founded an urban festival series bringing top scientists together with artists, athletes, businessmen and leaders to share cross-discipline solutions to global and community ills.

He then became Executive Producer for the Clean Energy Tour, a statewide "Get Out The Vote" music tour backed by 120 organizations, reaching over 200 thousand youth on 8 college campuses. The renowned director, James Cameron, read a message written by Aaron on behalf of the biosphere. In the wake of the Haiti earthquake, he was asked to travel to Port-Au-Prince to advise a food-security initiative by employing music and storytelling as a way to give voice to marginalized communities in the challenging rebuilding process. It was then that his long-time oral storytelling project, Pacha's Pajamas, emerged as a prime tool to explore nature-themed issues through music and storytelling.

An award-winning educator, artist and entertainer, Aaron Ableman has dedicated his life to serving children, youth and families. Ableman has worked and/or performed with artists including Mos Def, Talib Kweli, Joan Baez, Q'orianka Kilcher, Earth Guardians and is a sought after entertainer around the globe. His life and work have been heralded in publications such as the LA Times, CNN, MTV, New York Times, MTV, Origin Magazine, Montreal Mirror, Climate Reality Project and the SF Examiner. Aaron is a CoFounder of BALANCE Edutainment and a consultant for numerous arts, education and environmental organizations.

Twitter: @ablemantra

Instagram: @aaronableman

Website: http://aaronableman.com

ABOUT THE ILUSTRATOR

Art has always been a major part of Allah's life. He attended the Academy of Art University in San Francisco.

He chose to study animation because he had already mastered the other forms of art at the school. He started out studying 2D animation. His skills impressed his instructors, the Lab Techs, and his peers. Next he delved into 3D animation with Maya. His skills were so advanced that he was allowed to skip several required classes.

After the intro class, he began producing his own animated shorts. His first film won an award at the AIGA World Studio Scholarship Program. He produced music videos honoring music legends, Michael Jackson and Tupac Shakur, which became YouTube sensations. The animation scenes that really interest Allah are action and comedic scenes. He does animation for gaming as well as feature animation. He handles all technical issues including lighting, rigging and rendering.

Allah has been the Animation Producer/Director for all of the animations in Animated Book. He says this about the his work on Pacha's Pajamas:

This work has a profound message based upon spiritual philosophies and and environmental awareness to which I'm connected. Which is why my heart and my creative input yields great inspiration to this project. When I first began working with the company as a freelance artist, I thought to myself, this is a great way to make some quick money.

Over time, however, more and more of the story was revealed to me. I realized this was the kind of work I'd been waiting for. When I produced this film it was designed with the intention to inspire, remind, and warm the hearts of all who bear witness. I feel humanity hasn't completely forgotten their connection to nature; we just need to be reminded, and that's what this work does.

BALANCE

BALANCE Edutainment is the Mixed Reality/EdTech firm that makes books come to life with augmented and virtual reality. BALANCE has produced the first-of-its-kind Animated book or ZBook, Pacha's Pajamas: A Story Written By Nature — which instantly grabs attention and makes kids want to read. Hovering our Pacha Alive ZBook app over the illustrations in the book brings them to life with animations featuring celebrities including Cheech Marin, Mos Def, and Cheech Marin.

BALANCE's intention with the Pacha's Pajamas series is inspire, motivate, and support young people in knowing themselves, becoming youth leaders, and making positive change in their communities. Pacha reminds us that we are all connected, we have everything we need within ourselves, and we can create the world we want to live in.

To learn more about ZBooks, visit balanceedutainment.com.

Imagination Heals brings transformational entertainment to Children's Hospitals, schools, and enrichment programs leveraging the therapeutic effects of music, stories and the arts to bring hope and inspiration to kids when they need it the most. The program has many benefits for children, hospitals, celebrities and sponsors.

"Music can reduce depression and anxiety, calm us down and offer relief for chronic pain." ~Kaiser Permanente

As its first offering, Imagination Heals distributes the nature-themed Pacha's Pajamas books and albums to selected hospitals for use in the hospital creative and gifting programs. The program also brings performances and celebrities to the hospitals. Performances include an interactive storytelling experience called the Pacha's Pajamas Story Cypher.

"Pacha's Pajamas music, books and shows will be beautiful gifts for our low-income youth!"
~ Nutritionist at Highland Hospital in Oakland, CA

imaginationheals.us

After Pacha's next dream adventure Foodlandia, you'll never eat the same again!

Pacha and her younger brother Paco visit a dreamworld where everything is made out of food. The emperor Hamburgoni and his minion fries have lanced the cantaloupe sun, which is changing the climate. Popsicle mountain is melting and broccoli forest is on fire. Will Pacha and Paco save Foodlandia in time for dinner?

Visit Pacha's website for videos, fun activities, and much more...
Also get your free copy of Pacha's Family Room Companion.

http:// pachaspajamas.com

The
PACHA'S PAJAMAS
Musical

Featuring

Cheech Marin as Señor   Yaasin Bey as Narrator   Talib Kweli as Butterfly

13 songs + 15 story tracks

14 Songs + 1 Story Track
+ 1 Mindfulness Track

Available at online retailers
pachaspajamas.com, and the Pacha Alive app

Experience Our App

Pacha Alive

* Virtual Reality (VR)
* Augmented Reality (AR)
* See Yourself in AR
* AR Gift Greetings
* Dance with Pacha
* Challenges
* Music
* Updates

Experience Our App

- Virtual Reality (VR)
- Augmented Reality (AR)
- See Yourself in AR
- AR Gift Greetings
- Dance with Pacha
- Challenges
- Music
- Updates

DATE DUE			
NOV 01 2018			
WITHDRAWN			

CPSIA information can be obtained
at www.ICGtesting.com
Printed in the USA
BVOW09s1946231117
500657BV00003B/5/P

9 781630 477042